Proxima Station

Book One of the Proxima Station Saga

MIKE MOLLMAN

Beaver Castle Media

Cover art by K. Francis
Character art by K. Francis and Dmitry Yakhovsky

No Gen AI was used for the cover art, the character art or the prose in this book.

Proxima Station
Proxima Station Saga, Book One

ISBN   978-1-958265-12-3   Hardback
        978-1-958265-13-0   Paperback
        978-1-958265-14-7   Ebook
        978-1-958265-17-8   Audiobook

DEDICATION

*I've used the names of many friends
throughout this book and none of the
descriptions herein resemble their true personalities.
Thanks for befriending this cantankerous old man.*

For free bonus maps, schematics and more
for all my works, visit my Substack page.

AuthorMikeMollman.Substack.com

Proxima Station

Book One of the Proxima Station Saga

United States Space Force

To: Benjamin Kahn, Ph.D.
     Head of Graduate Studies
     Anthropology Department
     New Jersey State University

Dear Dr. Kahn,

It is imperative that the Ph.D. defense of Mr. Anthony Bell occur no later than Friday, April 7. His specific expertise on diverse peoples, such as the !Kung tribe of Owambo, Namibia is needed for a matter of some importance. The safety of the United States of America may depend upon your adherence to this request.

Because of the outstanding nature of your graduate program, lucrative future grants are being considered as well as access to an exclusive military program for anthropologists. We are all patriots who serve in different ways. The call has been made for you to step up or the good of your country.

Kate Janeway

Kate Janeway, Col, USSF
Nellis AFB, NV USA

Table of Contents

Chapter One

The Defense

Why does Dr. Ben insist on a meeting on a Tuesday morning at the ungodly hour of seven thirty? I already finished my dissertation three months before I have to defend, and I'm not due to teach a recitation until tomorrow afternoon.

I swipe to open my calendar, making sure not to cut my finger on the crack running down the center of my phone. Nope, I don't have teaching assistant duties either.

I duck into the Butts Building, out of the miserable rain that's been falling all week, and can't help but smile.

I'm such a child.—Butts, haha. What am I, twelve?

Why in God's name would he insist on a seven thirty meeting?

The lights are on in the grad school office, so I greet Mrs. Laura Huie as I turn the door handle. Everyone calls her the dragon lady, though I've no idea why. She does tower over me, but I like to think of her as the nicest of Amazonian warriors.

"Oh good, I was afraid you wouldn't make it in before noon," she says, rising from her chair.

"I didn't think that was an option after the third time Dr. Ben called me this morning."

She waves her hand at me dismissively. "Go right in. He's in such a state already."

"What's this about?"

Laura shrugs. "Usually he'll tell me, but he's been mum on this one."

I put my finger next to my temple, acting like I'm shooting myself as I lean up against Dr. Ben's door and turn the handle.

"Good morning, Dr. Ben."

"Anthony, finally. Close the door and have a seat."

I try to make myself comfortable, but it feels like the silence before the guillotine falls. Dr. Ben locks the door.

Definitely don't like that.

He takes his reading glasses off and sits behind his desk. Then he absently puts them back on as he opens his desk drawer.

What is going on? It feels like I'm in an Indiana Jones scene.

"First, thank you for coming in so early. I know it's not your preferred time."

I grunt in agreement since all of a sudden, I'm too nervous to speak.

"Yes, well, let's get straight to it." He holds a single sheet of paper two feet from his face, tilting his head up to read it before handing me the smudged letter. "Can you enlighten me on this?"

I scan the letter. "Why is Space Force contacting you?" I ask. "Is this a prank? Where even is Nellis Air Force Base?"

"Those were my thoughts yesterday when I received this letter. In fact, I threw it away. Then at dinnertime last night, Provost Zunnoor called me at home and asked if I'd acted upon the letter yet. It turns out Nellis Air Force Base is near Las Vegas."

"Okay . . .."

"This colonel, Kate Janeway, her office already called the Dean of Arts and Sciences and the Provost to find out what action has been taken."

"Aunt Katie? What does she have to do with this?"

"You do know something about this."

"No, I don't know anything. My Aunt Katie, Kate Janeway," I point at the letter, "is my dad's sister, but I haven't spoken with her since, I don't know, my sophomore year of college?"

"So, you can't shed any light on why the !Kung culture is a matter of national security? Why are we all of a sudden interested in Africa again?"

"I have no idea."

"None?" He asks, incredulous.

"The !Kung are former nomadic pastoralists, who changed to more permanent settlements less than a hundred years ago and now they've been introduced to cell phones. Why would my documenting their cell phone habits be of interest to the military?"

"You know Area 51 is near Nellis," Dr. Ben says.

"Area 51? You mean the space alien dissection place that all the wackos talk about?"

"Sounds like something Space Force would take an interest in," Dr. Ben says.

"Is this a prank?" I look around his office for anything out of place.

Dr. Kahn ignores me. "Never in my life have I heard of anything anthropologically related being critical to the national interests." He looks at me. "Did the !Kung tribe all of a sudden find alien technology?"

Does he expect me to answer?

He slumps back in his chair. "Apparently our university is in line to receive an eight-figure grant for an unannounced project according to Usman Zunnoor. Have you ever spoken to the provost?"

"No, sir."

"Well, Usman is quite forceful in normal conversation. He has a very direct and slightly threatening manner about him. He informed me and the rest of your graduation committee that you'll be defending your dissertation this week."

"What?"

He holds up his hand to stop me from babbling half-formed thoughts. "After consulting with everyone, you'll be defending tomorrow at ten."

"You didn't consult with me!" I start pacing in Dr. Ben's ridiculously small office. The Butts Building is a hundred years old, and it's never seen anything as weird as this, I'd wager. The wooden floor creaks with my every step.

Even the building is laughing at the situation.

"Your dissertation is finished, right?"

I plop into the chair. "I mean, I guess. All the arguments are there, but I wanted to go over it another time or two."

"I'm scheduled to defend on July 21st. And anyway, the letter said by April seventh." I point unnecessarily at the letter.

"Yes, as Provost Zunnoor quite clearly informed me last night, and the entire dissertation committee, for that matter, that if you should be unsuccessful, you will have another try on Thursday and again on Friday, if needed. He's basically told us that we have no choice but to pass you."

"What is happening?" I look at the corners of the ceiling. Surely there are cameras recording my disbelief.

"Furthermore," Dr. Ben says, lowering his head to peer at me from overtop his reading glasses, "the provost invited—though I doubt he had any real choice—a member of Space Force to be present during your defense."

"Do I get a say in this?"

"You really don't have any idea about this?" Dr. Ben asks.

"I don't quite believe it now."

My mentor stands and takes his glasses off. "Well, Anthony, I'd advise you to go over your dissertation as many times as you need before tomorrow morning."

* * *

The thermostat doesn't work in the conference room, to no one's surprise, so the tiny room packed with six people is sweltering for my defense. It's like I'm back in the Kalahari Desert, except no one here is as welcoming as my hosts in Owambo were.

True to their word, there is a member of Space Force standing at the side of the room. There's a chair for Lieutenant Colonel Melissa Stone, but she's declined it, twice. I guess the military makes you an expert at standing and waiting. She's a rigid woman, about my age, who has yet to show the faintest bit of emotion.

She seems like a charmer.

Dr. Carter is sitting closest to her, and he gives her frequent, uncomfortable glances before he starts playing with his wild gray hair again. More than once, I've had the misfortune of using the restroom during his hair teasing sessions. Why doesn't he just lick his finger and stick it into an electrical socket? It would be much quicker.

I take a breath and look at the floor. It's almost showtime.

* * *

The defense is a blur, and even now I have very poor recollection of it. I remember being uncomfortably hot, and some back and forth between Dr. Ben and Barry Carter. I was sent out of the room, and Colonel Stone was instructed to leave as well, but she didn't. I'm still not sure why. She had no right to be in the room during the deliberation.

Here I sit, outside the room, trying to remember what I even said. There are muffled voices from inside, but I can't make out a single word. A hundred years in this building and they've developed the perfect torture method. At least it's cooler out here.

The doorknob jingles and I immediately sit up straight. Dr. Ben pops his head out. "Please join us." Then he disappears, though the door is left ajar.

As I push the door inward, the hot, sweaty air hits my face and, for an instant, I consider running away.

Ah, the fight-or-flight response.

My mentor gives me a smile. "Dr. Bell, congratulations."

I freeze as my brain tries to process those words. If not for Dr. Ben's handshake, I might still be frozen in place. The others shake my hand and I dumbly smile and say thank you to each of them. Barry Carter walks around the scrum, giving me a death glare as he leaves.

Thanks to the lieutenant colonel's presence and the sweltering heat, Barry Carter's soaked hair is stuck to the sides of his head. Yeah, I don't know what's going on in my life right now, but watching the old blowhard get deflated will forever be a cherished memory.

In the end, Dr. Carter declined to approve my defense, making the final tally three to one in my favor. I'm still irked by the no-confidence vote. When's the last time someone defended and the outcome wasn't unanimous? Still, as of today, I am officially Anthony Bell, Ph.D.

"Gentlemen," Colonel Stone says, "please give us the room."

"I'll gladly leave this sauna," Dr. Ben says, before anyone can complain. One by one, the people I feared most I my life leave the room.

That whole ordeal is over and I feel robbed of any sense of relief. The colonel slides the pages of my dissertation to the end of the table. An avalanche of two hundred plus pages, detailing all of my hard work, tumbles to the floor. She doesn't even acknowledge it.

"I have documents for you to sign."

"What kind of documents?"

Silly me, I thought my defense would be the most anxiety-inducing event of the day.

She lets out a short breath of air and glares at me. Thanks to her glasses, her eyes look two times too big. "You just got the most worthless degree known to man and I can't even fathom how much debt you incurred to get it. This opportunity will pay off your student loans and give you a stable income."

I focus on her silver star thingy on top of her left shoulder as she sets the paperwork out in two piles.

"You can't be wasting time; we have a plane to catch."

"We do?"

She mumbles her disdain while fishing for a pen inside her attaché.

"What is that insignia?" I ask.

"It's a silver oak leaf. It means I'm not someone to be trifled with." She grabs the first sheet of paper and thrusts it into my hands.

"Am I being sworn into some sort of secret military society?"

"Yes," the lieutenant colonel says without looking up. "These are non-disclosure agreements. They basically say if you ever talk about what you're going to do, we can throw you in Leavenworth and forget about you. Now hurry up and sign or we're going to be late."

"What is Project Giant Step?" I ask. "Did you find a Yeti?"

Her coal-black eyes fix on me. "Sign. The. Papers."

I break eye contact. God, she's a scary woman. I'd rather face an angry linebacker.

I race through the stacks of paper. I might be signing my life away, but that's a problem for another day. Right now, I feel like I'd spontaneously combust, except for the oppressive mugginess.

"What should I call you?" I ask.

"Lieutenant colonel or ma'am."

I go over the details I gleaned during my speed signing. I don't know anything about anything yet, so I don't think me getting shot is likely, for now.

"What did you do in Africa?" the lieutenant colonel asks.

"I just spent two hours discussing it—you were present the whole time."

"In English, what did you do?"

"I documented the changes in the !Kung people of Owambo, Namibia as they transition from a farming community to a ranching society and ultimately to one with cell phones, thereby giving them access to the wider world."

"That's it?"

"Well, it's of great interest to anthropologist like me who subscribe to historical particularism theories. Every society develops in its own bubble. With the advent of cell phone use, that bubble is bursting in Owambo. Me being there to document the change will give us a better insight into societal adjustments during periods of rapid technological and sociological upheavals to a society's cultural framework."

"Good," the lieutenant colonel says as she gives the paperwork one last tap on the table. I think I was just background noise while she double checked all of my signatures. Once the pages are put away, the lieutenant colonel opens the door. "There's a car waiting for us outside."

"Where are you taking me?"

"McGuire Air Force Base."

There's a black SUV with dark windows parked illegally on the sidewalk directly in front of the building. Of course, there's no parking police around to see this, but park without a paid permit for more than fifteen seconds any other day and wham, it's a thirty-five dollar ticket.

"How long will we be gone?" I ask.

"Years, hopefully," she says as the doors lock.

"What about my car?" I can't even fathom what the parking fees will be.

Am I going to owe an amount equal to my student loans when I return?

"Your father will take care of it."

"But I have the only set of keys."

She looks at me with something approaching pity, like I'm a wide-eyed freshman stepping on campus for the first time. "That's adorable. Go," she tells the driver.

Colonel Stone looks out her window as we depart. She's obviously not going to tell me anything. I take out my phone and start playing minesweeper. It's a stupid game, but it gives me something to do.

"I'll take that," the lieutenant colonel says as she swipes my phone. Before I can protest, she smirks at me. "You agreed to give up all recording devices."

"I did?"

She turns off my phone before it goes into the attaché case with the papers.

The SUV takes the turnpike to Mount Holly Road. The driver slows and flashes his ID at the guards. They wave us through the gate. Our driver doesn't stop again until we're on the tarmac.

"That's our ride," the lieutenant colonel points to a gargantuan gray plane.

"You could fit my parent's house inside that."

"They live here, in New Jersey?"

"Yeah," I say.

"Probably two of their houses, then." She turns to the driver, "take us over." She tosses me a pack of ear plugs. "Put these in."

The driver stops next to the ramp at the rear of the plane where a military member in an olive green flightsuit directs us up the ramp. I look up at the enormous, growling engines. Even with the earplugs, the steady roar of the engines is impressive.

"When will it take off?" I shout.

"Once we're situated."

"I only have the clothes I'm wearing. When can I go back to my apartment and pack?"

"We'll supply you with everything you need," the lieutenant colonel yells.

"Am I being sent to some secret torture site?"

That's the first time the lieutenant colonel smiles. "Something like that, but it's supposed to have amazing views."

"What is this all about?" I motion throughout the plane.

She points, "have a seat there on that pallet."

My seat is covered in cargo netting and the least uncomfortable way to sit down makes it feel like I'm wearing a thong. The ramp closes, and the loadmaster tells us it will be wheels up in two minutes.

The lieutenant colonel relaxes finally. I mean, she still looks like an uptight school marm from the eighteen hundreds, but it's an improvement.

"Remember, you cannot repeat any of this unless you want to spend the rest of your life at Fort Leavenworth. I'm sure Kansas is lovely in the winter," she yells into my ear.

At least, I think that's what she said over the roar of the engines. She sits on the edge of the pallet and shouts loud enough to be heard.

"On February 28 of this year, an alien race landed on the salt flat of Dry Groom Lake; you would know it as Area 51. The race, known as the Bwetnibs, invited us to join them and four other spacefaring species on their space station orbiting Proxima Centauri b."

"For real?" I shout at her. She doesn't seem like the kind to play a prank, but . . ..

The whole plane shifts underfoot as it starts to move.

"The Bwetnibs are an engaging species and they apparently have a translation device embedded somewhere under their skin."

"What do they look like? Are they little green men with big heads?"

The lieutenant colonel stops and stares at me for a long moment. "This will go faster if you keep your mouth shut and listen."

I lean in closer to her and place my hands in my lap. She doesn't seem like the type to repeat herself.

"We have confirmed that no other governments are aware of the visit. It was only after the aliens monitored our airwaves for six months that they settled on Area 51, since there have been alien visitations there in the past."

"Have they? I mean other aliens. Have they landed there before?"

She glares at me until I break eye contact and look down at my feet. The plane starts speeding down the runway. I'm facing backwards, and that always makes me queasy.

"The five species are the Bwetnibs, the Yetis, the Napoleons, the Erati and the Umbrans. You will get briefed on them at Nellis."

"You're telling me there are five other intelligent species out there?"

"Yes, and with your background in anthropology, you will be responsible for meeting with them on a daily basis, evaluate them, and report your findings to the station command."

"What findings? What am I supposed to focus on?"

"Their technology, how to manipulate them, their weaknesses," she says. "Whatever the brass tells you to uncover."

"Are there species at Area 51?"

"No. A Bwetnib ship will be leaving on the eighth for Proxima Centauri Station."

"They just landed one day out of the blue?"

"No, the first time they landed was in Las Vegas. Fortunately, we were able to pay some dwarfs to dress like them and explain it as a crazy alien costume for the tourists to have their pictures taken with."

"Um, I believe the term 'little people' is preferred."

"Are you telling me what the aliens prefer?" Our noses are nearly touching.

I rub my gurgling stomach. "No ma'am. I was saying that 'dwarfs' is an offensive term, for short humans."

Her eyebrows nearly touch as she scowls at me. If there's an afterlife, hell will be afraid to take her.

"You got three hours. I suggest you sleep."

Dr. Anthony Bell

Anthony Bell

Age:	28
Sex:	M
Occupation / Role:	Anthropologist
Social Status / Rank:	Specialist
Height / Build:	5'11" (1.80 m)
Weight:	210 (95.3 kg)
Hair color:	Brown
Eyes color:	Brown
Marks/Tattoos:	None
Education / Training:	Ph. D in Anthropology
Skills/Talents:	TBD

Chapter Two

Out of this World Education

It's already hot today, and it's only nine in the morning, or oh nine hundred, as everyone here says. I've been assured, even by Nevadan standards, today is especially hot for early April. My sweat evaporates as soon as it's formed, leaving tiny salt crystals clinging to my face. It's our final day of briefings before we get on the ship and head for outer space.

I don't know if Aunt Katie pulled strings or not, but this morning we each got a single ten-minute phone call, supervised, of course. Dad answered the phone when I called, like he was expecting it. He normally lets everything go to voicemail, even me. He already knows where I'm going, so there's no need to tap dance around my mission. He takes the lead and asks me how the defense went and how I'm holding up. Basically, he doesn't give me a chance to ask any questions.

Dad tells me to call Aunt Katie "Gillis" just before the line goes dead, which is so like him. He timed the whole thing perfectly so we couldn't say goodbye.

I didn't even get to ask about my car! The more I think about it, I don't care. They can keep it. What I really want to know is what's up with the name Gillis. I guess Aunt Katie is going to have to tell me.

In the three days we've been here, none of us has left the administration building except to go to the dining hall and the dorm. Everywhere I go I'm escorted. Even if I go to the latrine, as they call it, someone follows me. It's like prison, except without the bars. Our warden is Major Ryan Patrick. The only thing interesting about the man is his eyes protrude like a pug.

I'm agnostic, but I pray that today be more like yesterday and less like the first day. Day one, Wednesday, was all about physics and engineering and specific technologies the higher ups want to discover. We all know they really mean steal technology, but they don't say the quiet part out loud. It offends their honor, I guess.

There's six of us in the briefings, though two of the guys haven't spoken a word. They're all biceps and crew cuts. I swear one of them fell asleep yesterday. My other three compatriots at least have definable skills.

All of my college science was the social science variety, so the physics went way, way over my head. I didn't fall asleep and that should totally count as a win. Hiram and Trinity and their debating technical details are always fun to watch, even if their questions are complete gibberish to me.

Hiram is a physicist, he says. He's always wearing camo, though, and talks a lot about guns. I guess he's either Army or Marines. I don't know what makes me more uncomfortable, physics, the military or gun talk. Hiram talks about nothing else, so we haven't really bonded. Also, what's up with the name Hiram? There's been like twelve people named that in the last hundred years. Did his parents know they were going to hate him at birth?

Trinity is a top-notch aerospace engineer. She's always in a pantsuit and her dark hair is tied up in a topknot, with the remaining hair wrapped around it, making her head look pointy. When she wears a wide-brimmed hat, which you have to do here, the center is always poking up. If she wore all black, she'd pull off a respectable witch's costume. She'd also melt into the ground because of the heat, so maybe not the best idea.

Her eyes would be pretty if they didn't have that 'I'm trying to bore inside your head' sort of intensity. I asked if the alien engines ran on dark energy, and her gaze never wavered from the side of my head, like I had more information tucked away. I was just trying to contribute instead of being a mannequin. It's not like I know about that stuff.

Creepy.

Yesterday was both better and more frustrating for Matt Sorenson and me. Matt looks like he belongs in a biker gang; bald head, tattoos everywhere and an eight inch curly black beard that he styles into a point. With enough hairspray, he could use it as an entrenching tool, as they call it here. I'd call it a shovel, but I'm not military.

As a vet, the animal kind, Matt is as interested as I am about life on the space station. He's the only one I've been able to relate to. He's here to learn about their physiology and I'm here for their cultures. I suppose the truth of the matter is, we're probably both here because we were volun-told and didn't have a lot of say in the matter. Regardless, it's way better than staring at equations like nerds.

Matt and I are gobsmacked that they can't even tell us what the homeostatic temperature is for the aliens. I mean, all you have to do is pull out a temperature gun, aim and press the button. Just that bit of information would give clues about their living conditions. Who do they have up on the station, anyway?

They also can't answer any of my simple questions, like the time it takes for each species to reach adulthood, if they are solitary or communal or any of a host of other very basic questions. Matt assures me they have to be communal to agree to live on a space station together, and I don't disagree. I just wish Space Force had answers to my anthropological questions.

When it comes to living on the station, well, that's something they have all kinds of data on. The air pressure is only seventy-seven percent of Earth's, but it has twenty-four percent oxygen as opposed to our twenty-two percent, so it's only noticeable at peak cardio. At least, that's what they tell us. The only exercise I get is lifting doughnuts, so I just file it away as a factoid to share later, whenever I'm allowed to rejoin society. The bicep guys are all uptight. I guess they're worried about workout regimes.

I ask the others why the muscle guys are in our group, but I only get shrugs from Hiram and Trinity. Matt shushes me and promises to tell me later. The way they zone out during the briefings, it's almost as if they're in need of a charge.

That's probably an insult to robots.

* * *

According to Matt, the two guys who don't talk to us are security, as in making sure whatever we learn remains within Space Force. So, internal spies, though we're not supposed to say that out loud either.

Today, everyone is excited. After the briefing, and I mean right after the briefing, we all board for Proxima Centauri. I don't know where that is, and it doesn't help that the star is in the southern plane of the night sky and too faint to see without a telescope. I mean, they showed us pretty pictures of a three star system and said we're going to the red one, but whatever else they were trying to get across was way over my head.

Watching the Milky Way extend from horizon to horizon these last two nights is not something I'll ever forget. For some reason, it just doesn't seem real with the sky as dark as it is, that the nearest star to our solar system can't be seen with the naked eye.

Dad would be so proud. All those times he dragged me outside in the middle of the night to see a conjunction of something and something else, and even the trip to the Arizona desert just to see the night sky, and now Matt, Trinity and I go out every night to gaze upon them. Both of them know the names of dozens of stars. I, on the other hand, remain silent, enjoying Trinity's explanations about what makes each star special.

* * *

"Gather around," he says. "This is the final briefing before launch at thirteen hundred hours."

I think the projector screen Major Patrick uses has been here since the base opened in the fifties. It's not even as wide as my wingspan, and if anyone should attempt to retract it, it would likely crumble to dust. The wall behind it is corrugated, but would probably make a better screen since the images would be bigger. The major reprises his monotone drone, which quickly fades into unintelligible background noise.

The six of us take our positions on either side of the screen. The first image is of a furry, dog-like creature with huge tusks protruding from its lower jaw and extending past its four eyes. It stands only waist high and has a huge, bulbous head; like as disproportionally big as the purported green aliens that capture and probe humans all the time.

"These are the Bwetnibs, the aliens that made contact with us here at Groom Lake."

"They have four eyes giving them unsurpassed stereoscopic vision over a range of one hundred and fifty degrees," the major says, "and they have two compound eyes on the sides. It is unknown what the visual acuity of these eyes are, but we do know that they have three hundred and sixty degree vision, so there's no sneaking up on them."

"Do you have an image of them looking straight on?" Matt asks.

Major Patrick silently clicks the button, yet somehow conveys his complete disdain. The straight on view is frightening. The teeth are yellowish and look like bars holding the face back.

"Sabretooth fangs!" one of the silent guys says.

"The mouth cannot open wide enough for the tusks to be useful. However, when they run, the weight of the head causes them to tumble. They literally perform forward rolls when going at top speeds. The tusks protect the face and give a rounded surface to continue the roll. By turning their heads to one side or another, they can change their direction, even at top speed."

"Do they have a nose?" Matt asks.

"It is located inside the mouth cavity."

Matt leans over to me. "I bet you anything they're processing smell as they roll. With movement like that, they'd be sampling different levels in the air column as they go."

I nod toward Major Bulging Eyes. "Why don't you tell him that?"

"Nah, I'd rather confirm it myself. It'll make my first report easy to write." He gives me a wink. "Gotta play the game."

"The Bwetnibs are, we believe," the major says, "the most simplistic of the aliens and the most likely to speak candidly about technology and other information."

"They're the ones that arrived here?" I ask, interrupting the major's monotone musings. "Using their own interstellar ship? And you think they're simplistic?"

The major gives me a cold look. "That's why you're being sent up, Bell. Command wants detailed dossiers on all the races, which should be your specialty, *Doctor.*" He doesn't wait for a response. "If you can tell us the best way to interact with them so that they'll share some tech with us, then you will have earned your very exclusive and expensive ticket."

Matt flicks my elbow and gives me an 'I told you so' look. "It's just about smoke break time, isn't it, Major?"

"Make it quick. You leave in forty minutes.

Trinity and Hiram huddle together, discussing significant figures, or whatever the math types do. The two silent guys go chat with the major. Neither Matt nor I smoke, but everyone's happier after these breaks.

"Did you hear that?" Matt asks. "You only have to keep it together for forty more minutes."

"There's a reason why I never considered the military."

"Just think, we'll be learning about five alien species in no time. I've got to find out what evolutionary pressures caused the saber-toothed fangs to develop. And the slug species! The Napoleons, I mean, how on Earth, whoops, can't use that phrase. How on their world did they become the dominant species?"

He continues to ramble, but I only half listen. It's why we get along. Each of us can give voice to our interests without being shushed.

"I found a scorpion in my shoe this morning!" I say, just remembering.

"I bet you're glad I told you to shake them out every time before putting them on." He continues rambling, but it becomes white noise to me.

Before I went to live with the !Kung, I studied their customs and mannerisms for six months. The first week, if not the first day, can make or break the whole immersion. Yet the military has provided only a few grainy pictures of each alien species and lots of unsubstantiated assumptions. With that limited information they have, it won't be hard to fill out the dossiers on the aliens, I hope.

"Sorry to interrupt. What were you saying?" My eyes automatically scan the area again. I'm desperate to see one green plant here, even a weed.

I won't miss this drab, lifeless hellhole. The dingy tan ground, the brown mountains behind the base, even the once white buildings that have become sandblasted into pitted beige constructions of despair. Only the dried salt lake has any color, and that's a dirty yellow. The next time someone makes fun of New Jersey, the garden state, I'll tell them about this abominable place.

"Hey!" I hit Matt on the arm a couple of times. "What's going on there?"

"That's the old U-2 hangar."

"Well, it's not abandoned, even if it is a ways from the rest of the base," I say.

"Ahh, ahh, that's . . . that's a Bwetnib!" Matt says as he yanks at my shirt.

I use my hand to shield the sun and squint in the distance. "Maybe," I say.

"I'm telling you, I saw the thing head on, and it saw me, because it immediately retreated into the hangar."

"If you two would like to rejoin the briefing," the major calls from behind us.

"I bet you anything they take us there after this," Matt says, his hands shaking. He looks at them, smiles at me, then holds his hands up at eye level.

I do the same, and my hands are shaking too. This is really going to happen!

"The next species is the Yeti, named because of the similarity between them and the Yetis here on Earth," Major Patrick says in a bored voice. "The Bwetnibs are the smallest alien. The Yeti are the largest."

I lean over and ask Matt. "Does he think Yetis exist here on Earth?"

He shrugs.

"Major Patrick," I call. "Is their name for themselves actually Yeti?"

"No, neither the Yetis nor the Napoleons' actual species names are pronounceable by us. The other three names are close enough for English speakers to get out."

Major Patrick drones on, disparaging each spacefaring species. According to him, despite their amazing technological achievements, none of them measure up to us humans. This guy comes straight out of the Victorian age, somehow missing the last hundred and fifty some odd years of progress. My bet is he'll never be allowed on the space station.

* * *

The major considers the Erati to be timid and clingy, like puppies. The Umbras are apparently filled with whatever their testosterone equivalent is, and they seek glory in gladiatorial combat. The Napoleons are nothing more than bureaucrats that look like upright slugs.

"These descriptions will obviously be updated by our *anthropologist,*" he says with... was that derision? It's hard to tell with Major Monotone.

It's a relief when he excuses himself. The silent guys get up and flex, er, I mean stretch in such a manner that their muscles bulge inside their skin tight shirts. Since they never leave each other's side, I've decided to call them Pete and Repeat.

"Who hurt Major Patrick growing up?" I ask.

The only useful information was the physical characteristics and pictures. Maybe that's why they showed us the pictures on the first day and again today. I'll be able to identify the species, which is something, I guess. No one knows if the aliens are social or solitary, tolerant of other species, or dismissive. The more Major Patrick talked, the more I think humans are the worst group on the station.

Can't be doing that.

The very last thing Dr. Ben warned me about before I left to study the !Kung tribe was not to think of them as noble savages. At first glance, any new culture looks superior to the one you come from, but that's because you're so familiar with your own culture that all you see are the warts. The invasive belief that cultures are objectively better or worse than one another is the bane of our world. They're just different systems used to maneuver through life based on the conditions in which you find yourself.

Matt makes for the smoking spot and instinctively, we follow him.

A dark SUV with two silver stars on the license plate pulls up to the building. A man jumps out of the passenger seat and opens the door for a diminutive woman. She may be short in stature, but she walks like she's a wolf among sheep. Wherever she looks, men and women straighten and hold their salute. Two other people leave the car and hurry to follow her into the reception area.

Matt whistles. "A two-star general. She has to be in command of this base."

"Get back inside and take your seats," Hiram says with urgency. Without waiting, he ducks back inside. Trinity, Matt, and I look at each other, then follow Hiram. Just as I take my seat, the short woman enters the room.

"Attention!" Major Patrick calls.

Hiram stands up straight. Pete and Repeat remain seated and unconcerned. Trinity, Matt, and I sit up straighter, but none of us know what to do.

"As you were," the general says. Another three people flow into the room behind her. At the doorway, a photographer is clicking away, mostly at her. Hiram retakes his seat, and the major looks a tiny bit less rigid.

"I am Major General Poppy Alexander and I want to offer some words before you begin your missions." She crosses her hands behind her back as she approaches us.

It's a gesture to put people at ease, though Hiram is sitting upright, not moving except to breathe.

"The aliens at the station can provide us with technology our best scientists can only dream about, or they can shut us out completely." She begins slowly pacing in front of us. "No one in human history has been given such a vital role. What you do up there will shape our culture, our beliefs and, most of all, our destiny for the next thousand years. It is vital that the staff at Proxima Station are our very best."

"Sir," an aide interrupts the general. "It's time."

General Poppy nods. "Failing to grasp this opportunity would jeopardize not only our place at the top of the world order, but our sovereignty as well. If anyone is slacking in their duties, we must know, *I must know*, immediately, no matter their rank. Is that understood?"

"Yes ma'am," Hiram replies.

"Major, please see to their deployment," the general says.

"Yes ma'am," Major Patrick says.

* * *

A new person comes to pick us up. I really should have remembered her name, but, well, that's what I do, forget names instantly. She's a chief master sergeant, that part I remember. Of all the people here, she's the only one willing to smile. She walks us to the old U-2 hangar, opens and holds the door for us. Her graying blonde hair glows in the noonday sun. For some reason, Samuel Clemens keeps popping up in my mind, but that was Mark Twain's real name and it has nothing to do with anything.

"Only onboarding people are allowed to enter here when the spacecraft is present," she says.

"So, we're really doing this?" Trinity asks with a nervous smile. "I have cleithrophobia," she blurts.

"I don't know what that is," our guide says.

"Cleithrophobia," Trinity prompts. "It's the fear of being trapped, like in an elevator, public restroom, places like that."

The hangar door opens and there's a sleek, silver spaceship waiting inside. The hull is perfectly smooth. The ship is bathed in light from above, yet not a single seam is visible. It's about as big as a school bus, but way more aerodynamic. Two short wings are on either side and a fixed rudder above. It kinda looks like the space shuttle from years ago, except sporty.

The six of us, plus the chief, stand just outside the hangar marveling at the ship. I'm suddenly hesitant to get on board. That ship represents adventure, sure, but also the unknown. An unknown too far ahead of our times to feel comfortable with.

"Do they fly this blind?" Hiram asks. "There aren't any windows."

Not helping, Hiram.

"What kind of stress will our bodies be put under while we're flying in that?" Matt asks.

"I've made three trips," our guide says matter-of-factly, "and I'm still standing. So if you want to make the trip, stop whimpering and get on board."

"Our ship doesn't look all that big," Pete says to Repeat. "I'm sure glad I don't have cleithrophobia."

Trinity grabs my arm in a death grip. "No," she says with hesitation. "It doesn't look very big at all."

"Partner up," the chief says, "and get on board."

"Hiram and I are ready," Matt says. He glances at Trinity quaking in her boots and gives me a 'you're so screwed' grin.

The chief extends her hand toward the hangar door. "Time to go on the adventure of a lifetime."

Trinity breaks away and leans against the doorframe. Her shoulders start rising and falling like she's run a marathon, at least, until she starts talking to the door. Her head starts darting this way and that as she yells 'stop it' and 'get a grip' to herself.

I know I should show some compassion, but the more I look at the ship, the more firmly I remain frozen in place. Part of me wants to run for it, and part of me wants to explore the unknown.

"I go on all the trips, but I don't leave the ship," the chief says. "I'm the most traveled human ever."

"Why would you do that?" The question is directed as much at me as it is her.

"Oh, I don't know. Maybe it has something to do with the fact that I can fix virtually any system I encounter. And maybe having a person like me on an alien spaceship for multiple trips seeing how everything works could prove helpful, but who can say?" She gives me an exasperated look.

That's what I needed, someone to talk about the ship in confident tones. I'm almost ready to board. "Aren't you worried about the cosmic rays and stuff?" They said something about them in our training, but I can't remember exactly what.

"How else would a Ms. Fixit want to spend her life? This is a dream come true." She looks over at Trinity. "Are you going to get her or am I?"

The chief is right, and it's exactly what I needed to hear. "I'll get her." I let out a long breath. I very easily could have been the one making such a scene.

"Good," she says oh so smugly.

Trinity is staring out the door at the clear, blue sky.

"Are you ready?" I ask.

"I think I am." She looks past me, at the ship. "It really is beautiful."

"It is."

Trinity latches onto my arm and starts with baby steps toward the ramp. Now that I'm her protector, any fear I have washes away.

We men are such predictable creatures.

The chief keeps up a low grumble as she urges us to hurry. "The ship is leaving at the prescribed time, whether you're on it or not."

"You can do this," I whisper.

Trinity keeps her head down, eyes shut, and she mutters to herself again. Once we're back on a level surface, she settles down into a neurotic person.

"Turn left and find your seats," the chief says. "Liftoff is only a minute away."

Trinity starts hyperventilating and, to compensate, she squeezes my arm even tighter.

If she passes out, I'll get use of my arm back.

"It's okay," I say in a soothing voice. "There are only a couple more steps to our seats."

The cabin has six huge, over-stuffed white leather seats, three on either side of the central aisle. Matt and Hiram sit in the back and it looks like they're being swallowed by their seats. The spy guys take the middle row, leaving the front two seats for us. I extract my arm and put the aisle between us.

I sink into the seat as if it were a giant beanbag chair made for sumo wrestlers. It conforms to my every curve, and the displaced cushion rises to form armrests. There are already armrests for the seat, but they're at nose level now and far enough apart that I can only reach them both if I stretch out my arms.

Are these seats made for the Yeti?

Looking to my right, all I can see of Trinity is her nose and her legs below the knee.

"Maddie Clements!" I blurt out. That's the chief master sergeant's name, and that explains why Samuel Clemens was taking up brain space.

"What?" Maddie calls from the ramp. She comes back to investigate. She's holding a dachshund under each arm.

I try to sink deeper in my seat and not make eye contact.

"Anthony called you," Matt says helpfully.

For an instant, I feel an irrational hatred for the man.

Maddie looks at me.

"Sorry, just nerves." I tug on the front of my shirt a few times. It's hot in here.

Fortunately, one of the wiener dogs squirms, drawing her attention away from me.

"Liftoff in five minutes," she calls from the corridor.

"These seats must have been designed to accommodate Yetis," Matt says.

"You're right!" Hiram says. "To think they'd fill the entire seat. I'm not in any hurry to meet one of them."

Trinity isn't the only one trying not to hyperventilate.

Sebastian Carlisle

41

Age:	6 months
Sex:	M
Occupation / Role:	None
Social Status / Rank:	None
Height / Build:	8 in (20 cm)
Weight:	16 lbs (7.3 kg)
Hair color:	Tan, smooth coat
Eyes color:	Brown
Marks/Tattoos:	None
Education / Training:	None
Skills/Talents:	None

Chapter Three
Ready to Launch

Hiram is lecturing Matt on acceleration and gimbals and exhaust deflection and who knows what else. Trinity is in her seat, nodding excitedly at each point, but not speaking.

At least she's distracted.

"Why are there dachshunds on board?" Matt asks as soon as Hiram pauses for a breath.

No one answers.

"What does Bwetnibian speech sound like, or any of the other languages?" he asks before Hiram can get going again. "It would be nice to greet them in their own languages."

He's right. Why didn't they include any of that? "It's weird that we didn't even hear—"

The hangar door raises, and I stop in mid-sentence. Effortlessly, the ship rolls out from cover and into the afternoon sun.

The mind blowing part is that from the outside, this ship looked completely solid. Now the "wall" next to me is letting in the light, but not the heat, from the scorching Nevada sun. I run my fingers along the glass-like substance and it's cool to the touch. Everyone is silent as we come to the realization that what we've been briefed on is actually going to happen.

Once outside the hangar, the window dims automatically. I can't see a single person outside. It's the hottest part of the day, but no one wants to see an alien spaceship? Or is everyone kept busy at this time so no one can see it?

The ship launches straight up and my butt sinks further into the seat. The acceleration is increasing, because, as I just learned, acceleration is a force, like gravity. Seeing my reflection in the window with my jowls being pulled down, I begin to resemble a bloodhound.

I look at Trinity, but only her calves and feet are visible. Turning back to the window, the blue sky darkens and my reflection, sagging cheeks and all, become more prominent. I shake my head, making my jowls sway left and right.

Yep, still a twelve-year-old at heart.

All at once, the acceleration stops, and I float in my harness. The pressure on my spine disappears and space giddiness takes over. I lift my feet and marvel that no muscles are needed to keep them floating above the floor.

"My hair!" Trinity says with delight.

Her mass of dark, wavy hair rises above her in a pattern that would make porcupines jealous.

"You have eighties hair," I say.

"We're now over sixty-two miles above Earth. Congratulations, you have all joined the spacefaring club," Maddie says.

Everyone cheers, except Trinity. She's pulled her legs up until her knees rest against her chin.

"It'll be okay," I say, and I mean it, but I'm too selfish to let go of my happiness, so it sounds incredibly insincere. I try to feel bad, but I'm in space.

Stars streak across my window at increasingly impossible rates. With a speed like this, could we even see Earth anymore? Trinity isn't the only one who's getting anxious. Only this tiny, little, air-filled box is keeping us alive. Out there, less than an arm's length away, our bodies would explode and frozen steam would fly in every direction, or something like that, if the movies are to be believed.

"Prepare for forward acceleration," Maddie calls over the intercom. "We'll be entering the wormhole in five minutes."

"Wormhole?" I say out loud. I was focused on the aliens and never did get around to asking what a wormhole is exactly. I glance over, but Trinity is still in the fetal position, so I shout back to Hiram. "What will the wormhole do to us?"

"Unknown!" he says with way too much enthusiasm. "It's all theoretical. It would require exotic matter to keep it open."

"What kind of exotic matter?" I ask.

"Not sure, but it would need to have negative mass."

"Isn't negative mass impossible?" Matt asks.

"Yes!" Hiram continues ranting, but I tune him out.

During our one and only phone call, Dad asked if I donated any of my little swimmers; just in case the wormhole does things to me. I guess he and Mom really want grandkids. There was zero chance of me asking anyone on base about that, and now I wish I would have. Great, leaving the only planet humanity has ever known, meeting five advanced races that can do who knows what to us, and now my ability to procreate is added to my worries.

Outside, it's the darkest black I've ever seen. Reflexively, I cover my nether region with my hands, because they'll protect me against exotic, negative mass matter type stuff. Sure, sure they will.

"For those of you sitting on the port side, Proxima Centauri b will come into view momentarily."

"What happened to the wormhole?" I ask.

"No one can explain it, but it freezes time, or something," Maddie replies over the intercom.

"Relativistic effects?" Hiram shouts.

"Um, yeah, sure," Maddie replies. "The station is in view now," she adds quickly, forestalling a theoretical physics conversation.

I smush my face against the glass. I don't know port from stern, but I'm going to check and see if I'm on the lucky side. A purplish planet comes into view. At the equator are the two continents. Each is a near uniform greenish-brown. North and south of each continent there are fluffy, soft-pink clouds.

"There it is!" Matt yells. "It's the tiny reddish-metallic thing just right of the equator."

"Why is the water purple and the clouds pink?" I ask. Not even at my most inebriated would I have believed I saw this. My question just hangs in the air, unanswered.

Hiram is the first to undo his restraints and join Matt at the window. No alarms go off, so the spy guys and finally Trinity follow suit. Trin's hand rests on my shoulder as she floats next to me.

"Ooh! So far down," she says, panic creeping into her voice.

"Hey, what's wrong?" I ask.

"I'm also acrophobic," she says, "afraid of heights."

She pulls herself down into my chair, which still has room to spare.

An attractive woman sits next to me and I can't even spare a quick glance her way. This might be the most unbelievable occurrence yet.

"Two, three, five, seven, eleven, thirteen–"

"What are you doing?" I ask as I force myself to glance her way.

"To calm myself down, I recite prime numbers in order."

"Um, okay. Can you tell me why the planet is purple and the clouds are pink?"

"It's the red light from Proxima Centauri. The purple is obviously water," Hiram cuts in. "The greenish-brown is a lush forest that covers the landmasses and the normally white clouds are pink because Proxima Centauri is a red star."

"I have got to go down there!" Matt says.

"Better you than me," I say.

"Is that the station?" a spy guy asks. It's the first time either of them has spoken in our presence. I'm not sure which one said it, but by definition, he has to be Pete, not Repeat.

"It sure is!" Hiram says.

The station is taking shape. Instead of a single point of light, it's lengthening and has numerous wheels along its axis.

Trinity squeezes my arm, so she must have looked and panicked again.

"It will be another two hours before we dock," Maddie's voice says over the intercom. "We're about to maneuver, which will send anyone outside their harnesses slamming against a wall or three. Take your seats for your final briefing before docking at the station."

The ship turns toward the planet and space station, removing them from our view.

Maddie comes back to our cabin and releases the wiener dogs. They bark incessantly as they float toward the back at a snail's pace. The short-haired one twists this way and that in a spastic dance. The long-haired one just sails by with a morose look on its face. Even Pete and Repeat are smiling at their antics.

Maddie proceeds to tell us the exact same facts about the other races that boring Major Patrick did. "That's the official briefing. What I'm telling you now hasn't been written down anywhere."

I sit up straight and listen. Finally, something useful.

"The Bwetnibs are regularly kicked, punched or otherwise struck by the Yetis and Umbras, resulting in them tumbling in forward rolls. They come across as innocent and quite simple, but remember, they built this ship and one of them is flying it, so don't fall for the act."

That wasn't anything like what I was expecting. I know of no culture on Earth that allows itself to be willingly manhandled. They clearly have an alien mindset. I can't explain why they would possibly allow it yet, but uncovering why is exactly what I've been trained to do.

"The next species is the Yetis. They are very simple. They are ten feet tall or more, primarily white in coloration and a complete mystery. They rarely speak, and when they do, it is usually only one or two syllables. We know nothing about them, not where they're from, how long they live . . . nothing. The other aliens have not volunteered any useful information on them either. It is believed that their taciturn nature is because they have little to contribute. They and the Bwetnibs are apparently the least intelligent of the species."

I shake my head at the assumptions being made. Shakespeare wrote, "give every man thy ear but few thy voice". Wouldn't that be a sign of high intelligence? We're on a ship made by the Bwetnibs and traveling over four light years farther from Earth than any manmade thing ever has. We're the dumb ones.

"The Umbras are masters of camouflage," the master chief continues. "They can change color and even the texture of their skin at will. The closest comparison we have on Earth are the octopodes. The Umbrans are roughly the same height as humans and they're the most openly curious of the five species."

I raise my hand. "Are any of these species known to be social, or are they more independent?"

Maddie waves my question away. I guess no one knows.

"The last species is the Eratis. Like the Umbras, they are similar in height to humans. They all wear a long shaggy coat with some sort of hybrid between fur and feather. A lot like a cassowary, if you know what they look like."

Does anyone have a clue what a cassowary is?

"Once they reach adulthood," the chief continues, "they shed this stuff, and it's woven into the mantle they all wear. Of all the aliens, they are drawn to jewelry and regularly wear hundreds or even thousands of dollars in gold and gems."

"What about the Napoleons?" I ask.

"The blobby bureaucrats?" Her nose wrinkles and she squints her eyes. "Just try to avoid them. We gave their race the name Napoleon for a reason. Virtually every interaction with them results in a complaint registered against us. They love their arbitrary rules. The good news is that they're typically desk bound. When they do move, they're slow as molasses."

Maddie shrugs her shoulders. "That's it. That's all I can tell you."

No one has even mentioned what languages are spoken, a single one of their customs, or what they eat. How long do they sleep? Don't know. Do they prefer hot or cold temperatures? Don't know. The list of unknowns is inexhaustible. What have they been doing for the last month?

I'm starting with poorly drawn conclusions and no detailed observations. I was so much more prepared when I went to live with the !Kung.

"Everyone will be given their dossiers for study, and someone from your group will be waiting for you at the docking bay," Maddie says. "Your luggage will be taken to your quarters for you."

"We're just now getting dossiers?" Hiram asks.

"Nothing in writing about the base is allowed to leave this ship," Maddie says. "The risk of this getting out is too great. So stop your bellyaching and read up while you have the time."

I have a million questions, but there's only one thought running through my mind.

I have luggage?

Dingle Barry

53

Age: 6 months

Sex: M

Occupation / Role: None

Social Status / Rank: None

Height / Build: 8.5 in (21.6 cm)

Weight: 19 lbs (8.6 kg)

Hair color: Tan, long coat

Eyes color: Brown

Marks/Tattoos: None

Education / Training: None

Skills/Talents: None

Chapter Four

The Space Station

The red light from Proxima Centauri is uncomfortable. Not that it aggravates the eyes, but just culturally, red symbolizes danger. I know everyone has to be anxious, but having their faces bathed in red light exaggerates the feeling. The star is on Trinity's side, but she refuses to look at it.

An astrophysicist who won't look at the stars. How did she even get selected?

It wasn't enough that Dad worked for NASA; he had to be an amateur astronomer too. He would drag me out with him. He used a red flashlight, because a regular one would ruin your night vision. Proxima Centauri feels like that, a dim, red light shining in your face.

"If you look at the right side of the star, and before you ask, yes, it is safe, you will see Proxima Centauri b again, this time as it transits across the face of the star. It only takes eleven days to complete an orbit, since it's eight times closer than Mercury is to the sun," the chief says.

"Won't the radiation kill us at that distance?" Matt asks.

"Weren't you listening during orientation?" Hiram asks. "The station has advanced materials to shield us."

But what about now, on this ship? Never mind, I don't want to know.

The planet's movement gives the illusion of a black circle moving across the star. It looks like a red death star slowly taking aim at us.

"Proxima Station, which is not the official name," Maddie starts, "is still bound up in committee, and likely will remain there for our natural lifetimes, is the single largest structure any human has ever laid eyes upon. Our vector will have us chasing the planet and we'll ultimately land with the sun at our backs."

"Can we see the station from here?" I ask.

"Nope. The star's glare is too bright. But our Bwetnibian pilot has agreed to take an image of the markings on the outside of the station. As our new linguist, that should be of particular interest to you."

"Um, I'm not a linguist," I stammer. "I'm an anthropologist."

"The marks are in the infrared part of the spectrum," Maddie says. "Four of the five races on the station—well, I guess four out of six now—can see them. Only we and the Bwetnibs cannot."

I want to go back to the linguist comment, but I don't know that I'll get anywhere with the chief. She's not even disembarking with us.

"I will be handing out your order packets now. Read up on your assignments. It will be fourteen hundred hours when we arrive. You are members of the station crew, and you have your orders."

I tear into my packet. I'm to report to human command, room three, at 14:15 hours. It's located at S1. I flip the page over. That's it. Report to S1 within fifteen minutes of arrival. Are they mad?

Where are my quarters? How do I get food? Where are the bathrooms?!

I check out everyone else. Trinity has a stack of fifty sheets of paper, covered in text and diagrams. Pete and Repeat sit quietly, amused at the rest of us. I guess goons don't have need of written orders.

Hiram's face is buried in his lap. By the sound of the shuffling papers, he must be speed reading his packet. Matt is taking a more leisurely approach. His sheets are all one sided. Each one has a picture in the top third, then a couple of paragraphs below it.

Matt looks up from his current sheet. It's an X-ray of an Umbran or Erati, I can't tell from here. He furrows his brow, then smiles. I hold up my single sentence of instructions.

His jaw drops, then he starts laughing at my predicament. I shrug. What else can I do? As everyone else devours their orders, I watch the tiny red star slowly get bigger.

* * *

That tiny red star has grown to be over three times larger than our sun, at least from our perspective. My brain tells me I should feel hot, but I don't. My eyes tell me it must be dusk, but it's not. I thought I had a good grip on this situation, but that's not true either.

Maddie informs us over the barking of the dachshunds that the hangar doors are opening. Since it's in front of us, we can't see the station, but the planet is right outside my window.

Light reflects off the bluish-purple water. The clouds have grown much darker and they blanket the continents. It must be one monstrous storm going on down there.

One of the few things they told us is that the planet is very similar to Earth. The big exception is that it lacks mountains and deserts. There are smaller islands well to the north and south of the equator, if they even use those terms.

"I have to get down there," Matt says, floating above my armrest. "My group is picking me up at the hangar and going to show me around the station. I don't report to duty until tomorrow at eleven."

I've been too lost in thought to even undo my harness. I hand him my one sentence order packet.

"Maybe S1 is close by," Matt offers.

"Maybe," I say, but I know better. That's not how Murphy's Law works. I change the subject. "Are we allowed on the planet?" I ask.

"Sure, all you need is a spaceship to take you," Matt says. "None of the aliens have volunteered to do so yet. Since you don't already have enough to do, linguist," he chuckles at my discomfort, "find out which alien species is most likely to take me down there."

The cabin darkens until the overhead lighting panels belatedly brighten.

"We will be landing soon. There will be some tight maneuvering, so buckle up or tossed around the cabin," the chief says over the intercom. "The gravity will vary from ring to ring on the station, but it will be ninety percent of Earth normal in the S ring, where the human quarters are."

"You better study up," I tell Matt as he navigates back to his seat. "I've already memorized my orders in their entirety."

There's a traffic jam of nerve impulses inside my head. The fear of meeting other intelligent species and for not being properly prepared is battling with whirling excitement. The main snarl in this gridlock, though, is my disbelief that this is even happening. And unlocking their cultures, their habits falls directly onto me.

They have to like me, or I'll get nowhere.

We hear a soft thunk as the ship sets down, and immediately gravity takes hold. Being weightless is fun, I guess, but I prefer firm ground under my feet, even if it's not ground, but metal, and I'm only a few feet away from instant death. Yeah, I need to stop thinking.

We settle down and wait for more commentary from the chief. As we wait, the harnesses disconnect and retract into our seats. I stand and look at the others. They're just as confused as me. The goons walk to the front of the ship without even looking at us.

"Follow them, I guess," Matt says. While everyone else gathers up their orders, I stare out the window. In truth, I don't like the spy guys and I don't want to be the one to stand next to them while we wait for the door to open.

Trinity gathers her papers and repeats Pete's and Repeat's steps. She's nice enough, but I'm waiting for Matt. Hiram hurries past me to compare notes with Trinity, no doubt.

Matt gives me a smile. "We are on a space station . . . in another solar system." He takes my hand and pulls me in for a shoulder to shoulder hug. His eyes are a little wild, but most likely, mine are too. "Remember, your number one goal is to get me a flight down to the planet." He taps his finger into my chest for emphasis. "I'll even name an algae colony, no," he gives me a big smile, "a slug after you. Yeah, definitely a slimy, detritus-eating slug!" His smile goes all the way up to his bulging eyes.

I bite my lip, then decide to release some pent up anxiety. "I should feel something, right? I'm having trouble processing the last few days, flying on a spaceship, the wormhole, now. I don't know what any of it means."

"I'd say it's just a case of mild shock." He slaps me on the shoulder. "Ask for a trip planetside to regain your bearings." He laughs and assumes his place in line.

Why am I the only person freaking out? Why am I standing alone in the cabin area?

Time to pull myself together. I have an urgent appointment to make.

I catch up with Matt outside Maddie's private cabin. Hearing her trying to quiet the incessantly barking dogs makes me happy. At least that's not one of my problems.

"Why?" I ask Matt, pointing at the door with the misbehaving dogs behind it.

The line starts moving out of the ship, so he doesn't reply. He's not pushing, but Hiram's personal space is definitely being violated.

Outside the ship, everyone finds their guides without issue. Hiram and Trinity are being led off to who knows where with their nerd clan, and Matt's people offer him a drink to celebrate his arrival.

Nope, not even a little jealous.

The goons are standing next to a grim-faced man with ominous dark eyes and a salt and pepper beardstache. Looking around, there's no one here for me. Looking up and down the hangar, I see nothing helpful, so I head for the cargo lift. Maybe there will be signage in English there.

"You're with me," the grim guy with the goons says. "I'm Tim Wolff and you're taking over for me."

Great, just the people I didn't want to be around.

"I have to report," checking my watch, "in fourteen minutes." At least I won't be around them for long.

"Follow me," Tim says, unconcerned, as he heads for the elevator. "First things first, our feet are in constant contact with the floor, but that's not gravity, it's centrifugal force. There are ten rings, each spinning around the central axle at different distances, which means each ring has a different force holding you to the floor. Unlike Earth, down is the outside of the wheel, up takes you to the central axle."

"Um, okay." I'm going to meet aliens in a couple minutes and he's talking about gravity, or not gravity, that other force. I stumble as I follow them and only just keep myself from falling.

They're going to think I'm hopelessly uncoordinated at this rate.

He points to an elevator and we all shuffle in. I feel much lighter here, almost as if I'm floating. I grab the handrail and pull myself down until my feet touch the floor. The doors close and as the elevator rises, my weight returns. Relieved, I release the rail and try to act normal.

The elevator slows, and my stomach rises. It must be all the stress. My gut's been out of sorts since Aunt Katie's letter. The elevator stops, but the spy guys and I continue upward. Tim is holding on to an arm rail and laughing at us. I get my arms up just in time to keep my head from smacking the ceiling.

"Point two," Tim says, "there's no gravity at the central rod, so you either hold on, use one of the harnesses attached to the walls, or crash into the ceiling.

Neither Pete nor Repeat got their arms up in time. Of course, if they get a concussion, how could we tell?

The doors open and Tim slides along the rail until he reaches the door. With a hand on each side, he propels himself out of the elevator. I let Pete and Repeat go first, so I know what not to do. Outside, Tim is looking at his watch.

"You have eleven minutes," he chides. "Point three, here in the rod, the top is command. The bottom, where we were, is the hangar. So top and up have different meanings here. Up and down are when you're on the wheels, top and bottom are when you're in the central passage. Got it?"

The other two nod, so I follow suit. I really wish he'd stop talking. I'm down to ten minutes left and I have no idea how long it will take to get to my meeting.

Tim leads us to a rounded pod car. Once inside, he slides into a harness and this time we follow his lead.

"It takes four minutes to get to the S level." He points at the goons. "You two will report for duty at reception. The two of us," he points at me and himself, "will have a conference with Colonel Janeway about the duties of our cultural liaison."

I swallow hard. Why did I believe I could do this? I can't even make pancakes reliably.

"Now listen to me," Tim says. "Your job is to profile the aliens so we can figure out how to gain access to their technology. Do that, and Earth will spring forward hundreds if not a thousand years technologically."

"All of Earth, or just the U.S. military?"

"We are the world's policeman," he says. "No one knows why, but all the aliens here are simpletons. Their tech is amazing, but talking to them is like talking to children." He frowns. "Maybe it's all the cosmic rays turning their brains to mush."

The ceiling in the elevator is twelve feet tall. It's definitely overkill for humans. There are mics stationed next to the doors at roughly three, six and nine feet. Six-inch images of a Napoleon and Bwetnib are next to the three-foot mic. A hastily drawn human stick figure is between what must be an Erati and an

Umbra at the middle mic. On the adjacent wall, a ten-foot-tall outline of a Yeti has its head even with the tallest mic.

Easy to guess which species was responsible for building the lifts.

"Do you really think your studying of the Kung tribes will give you special insight that the rest of us don't have?" Tim asks, disbelieving.

That's a tad bit aggressive, considering I've only just stepped foot on the station, and I can't stand bullies.

"It's the *tock*-Kung tribes," I say. "The exclamation point in front of Kung denotes a guttural click, like the tock in the ticktock noise we all made as kids," I say, like I'm talking to a know-nothing freshman.

"Great, your specialization in toddler amusements will be an asset, no doubt." He shakes his head and looks at the floor.

The pod-car thing starts out really slowly, but the speed is picking up now. My feet are being pressed against the floor well above what I'd feel on a normal elevator.

"Listen, the guys on the Interspecies Cultural Council will ask you questions relentlessly if you let them, so it's better that you're assertive from the beginning. You can do that, right?"

"I trained for deflecting questions before I left for my mission to Namibia."

"Wonderful," he deadpans. "All military questions from the aliens are off limits, as is any gossip you hear about our fellow humans."

"Do you mean to keep this from just the aliens on the council or them and the other humans?"

"First off, you will be the only human on the council, so no, I don't mean humans. Second, whatever you do, don't call them aliens."

The doors open on S1, but Tim doesn't move.

"I've been trained in interrogation techniques, and I've managed to get nowhere, so we don't expect you to do much between now and being sent back to Earth."

"You didn't try electroshock?" I feint surprise.

Tim gives me the 'one more comment like that' look. "Yeah, go in there making baby noises. I'm sure it will be successful. The next ship leaves in a week. If you don't have results by then, you'll most likely be on it."

He undoes his harness and opens the glass door to our pod. He pushes off gently and does a half flip, so his feet are leading. He lands easily and signals for us to hurry. The spy guys launch themselves from the pod and hit the floor gracefully. They both end up on their feet and smirk at me. I copy their example and let the gravity grab hold as I approach the outside of the ring. I've over-rotate and land on my hands and knees.

The corridor's floor feels spongy, like a running track. The temperature is warm, but it's a dry heat, as the saying goes, and nowhere near as bad as Nevada. Tim and his two goons break into a very fast walk, and I do my best to catch them.

I try to peer through the glass windows as we pass, hoping to see my first alien.

"We humans have to stick together. You know we were only allowed to join the station provisionally, right?" Tim asks.

"Um, no. No one on Earth knows about this place."

"Good, but you've just told me about Earth politics, which you are not to do. So be more mindful about what you say. If all else fails, channel the Yetis and say *nothing*."

He turns the corner abruptly and one of the spy guys and I run into each other. I bounce off him as if he were a wall.

"We have to present a united front," Tim continues, "so there can be no disagreements among us and no contradicting each other, at least until the one year evaluation period is over."

"They're more advanced than us. Can't they kick us off whenever they want?"

"Nah, the Napoleons adhere to the absolute letter of the rules. It'll take a couple of years to work through all the objections we would make. Besides, it would be easy to get the others to vote for us, out of spite for the little slugs.

The spy guy and I nearly collide again as Tim takes another sudden turn at the intersection.

"Oh, this is important. If you sleep with someone on the station, they will all know about it the next day. We don't know how, whether it's surveillance or leaks among the humans, but somehow they know. And that means that everyone will know within a day, so relationships tend to be the one night variety."

"With all that's happening, relationships aren't even on my radar."

He smiles at his guys. "That'll change. There are no weekends here. Just work and whatever amusements you can find at night." He grins back at me, like we're schoolmates or something.

"And your aunt is Colonel Janeway?"

"Yes, though I don't understand–"

"Whatever you do, don't mention that you're related to her to the aliens," he looks directly into my eyes, "under any circumstance."

"Um, why?"

"Just trust me. I told them my sister worked here, and she threatened to kill me less than thirty-six hours later."

"And that was because of the aliens?"

"What'd I tell you? Don't call them aliens!"

"But you just did."

"That's different. They would interpret what I said as if I was talking about one of the other species, not theirs."

I shake my head. "That makes no sense."

"It does," Tim says. He smiles as if he's told a joke. "Listen to me; I'm starting to sound like a Yeti."

I check my watch. I'm supposed to report in two minutes. "Is there anything else I should know?"

"Relax, the meeting is with me and your aunt. We have low expectations of you, so it will be hard for you to disappoint, though you may manage it."

The doors to human command are twelve feet tall and the Space Force seal is spread across both doors. It's a little crooked, and looks ridiculously small, but hey, it denotes mankind's first interstellar outpost.

The doors slide open and the guard inside stands up as we enter.

"McKay, Anderson, go see Youngblood over there. He'll get you set up," Tim says without breaking stride.

I guess I'll have to call them Pete McKay and Repeat Anderson.

I follow Tim through the door opposite the entrance and down a long branching hallway. He checks his watch before opening the door.

"Sorry, the kid was like a country bumpkin getting off the ship," Tim says.

"Tony! How are you?" Aunt Kate says.

"It's Anthony," I say as I pull on the bottom of my shirt, "and I'm fine."

"Well, I'm glad I took Rosaire's advice and had you come. Have a seat." She gestures to the lone seat on my side of the table. Tim walks around and sits next to my aunt.

"We don't have much time before your first shift," Tim says, "so we wanted to go over your objectives."

Aunt Katie pats the top of Tim's hand.

"We've been given a one year trial on this station. We only arrived here twenty days ago, so the timing is tight. Do whatever you can to ingratiate yourself with the aliens and see if they'll give us any details about their advanced technology."

"What happens after the year's up?" I ask.

"The Napoleons have already scheduled a vote on that day to determine if we can stay. I think we will, but better to plan for only one year."

"You will be stationed with the Interspecies Cultural Council, which meets daily for four hours," Tim says. "During that time, one representative from each alien race will be present."

"We've tried to get them one on one for more private conversations, but each has balked so far. That's why I asked your father about you coming here," Aunt Katie says.

"I am twenty-seven years old, not a child. You need to come to me, not my parents."

Tim makes a show of looking at his watch. "This babysitting session has been fun, but you have to hurry if you want to make your first council meeting on time."

Aunt Katie frowns at Tim, but stands up and walks around the table. She gives me an awkward hug, like she hasn't tried the maneuver in years. "Do your best. We'll debrief you after the shift is over."

"I will, Aunt Gillis."

She pulls away from me and cocks her head before a slow smile forms. "Only your father can call me that, and only when he's out of my reach."

Tim points at his watch. "Tick tock Kung man."

* * *

Tim doesn't say a word to me until we exit the lift on the C level. He sees me eyeing my watch. "Stop dawdling, you can't be late; the little Napoleon slug will never stop howling about it.

"I'm one step behind the pace that you're setting."

The gravity here, or centrifugal force, whatever it is, is way less than the human ring. My first few steps had me leaping like five feet high and nearly hitting my head. I notice that Tim makes short hops, almost like he's skipping, and I mimic his moves. Now if we just had people behind us beating coconut shells together, we could be in a Monty Python sketch.

Maybe I should call Tim the enchanter.

"Okay, here are the highlights," the enchanter says. "Stay away from the Umbras as best you can. Their breath smells like wet possum fur – do not ask me how I know that. The Bwetnib's breath is worse, but he's going to stick close to you, so there's not much you can do other than avoid leaning down. Just don't gag. Are you good at holding in your vomit?"

"I don't know."

"Well, do the best you can. The Erati will get jealous if you stick too close to the Umbras, which is another reason to keep your distance. Whatever you do, *do not* bring up protocols to the Napoleons. If it were me, I would rather kiss a Bwetnib, and unfortunately that has happened to me. Bleck! I've been trying to get a replacement ever since. You will not believe what I had to do to get you here."

"What?" I thought Aunt Katie pull the strings. Is he gaslighting me?

"I still have vivid nightmares." He shudders, ignoring my question. "If you can get a Yeti to say three sentences in a row, you'll get free drinks for a week from the human contingent, but then us spooks will ask you to repeat it a million times, so it might not be worth it." He shrugs before increasing his hopping rate to a canter. "I don't look forward to that, but it's your call."

I check the time. It's one minute before my shift.

"Oh, right, last thing, you'll be best off if you get the group to go on a patrol of the station. Sitting in one room with them for four hours should be avoided at all costs. Now hurry and get in there!"

74

Buddy

75

Age:	Unknown
Sex:	M
Species:	Bwetnib
Social Status / Rank:	Parade mate (?)
Height / Build:	3 ft (91.4 cm)
Weight:	51 lbs (23.1 kg)
Hair color:	light gold
Eyes color:	Black, compound eyes iridescent
Marks/Tattoos:	None
Education / Training:	Unknown
Skills/Talents:	Pilot, high priority for technology

Chapter Five
The New Chew Toy

Tim waves his hand in front of the doors and they soundlessly open. I hurry in to the darkened room. Thanks to me rushing, my hop sends me sailing ten feet inside.

Please don't let me stumble into one of my colleagues.

"Hey!" Tim shouts. "Don't be late for the debrief at the end of your shift."

"Wait, where?" I call.

He waves as the doors close, sealing me to my unknown fate. The lighting is dim and slightly reddish. I look around, but there's nothing but a dimly lit vestibule. No furniture, no artwork, just an eight foot wide hallway and a whole lot of empty space.

There's clacking noise coming from the other end, and it's getting louder. At the end of the hallway, the lights cut on and a blurry, reddish wheel-like thing turns the corner and rolls at me. I bend my knees and get ready to dive out of the way. I do my best to not tense up, but fail miserably. It slows, then stops ten feet in front of me. If it was any closer, I'd be colliding with a wall right now.

The creature stares between its two upturned fangs with four beady, black eyes.

"Hello?" I say as I bend down to take its outstretched paw? Hand? Whatever it's called.

"Youmustbe the new human," it says.

I blink at the thing while processing what it just said. "I am. My name is Anthony," I say slowly.

"I'lltelltheothers that you are here. Wedon'twant Crighton lecturing us on proper etiquette again."

Before I can ask his name, he's turned and is running away. His head sinks lower and lower as he runs until he's tucking into a forward roll. Just like Major Patrick said, it turns the corner without stopping its run-tumble.

That was a Bwetnib!

I freeze in place as my brain tries to process my first alien encounter.

Did I handle that right? Should I have asked his name? Told him that I come in peace?

The excitement has me all wound up, and man oh man, my mouth is dry and I have a sudden urge to pee. Where to relieve myself will *not* be the first question I ask another intelligent species! That settled, I wait and listen.

Do I follow him?

There's no other sights or sounds, though the way he left is now illuminated. The walls are maybe white? With the lighting so dim, it's hard to say for sure. I cautiously creep.. *no*, I amble down the path taken by the Bwetnib. There's conversation ahead. And it's all in English?

I thought there weren't any other humans?

Turning the corner, there is a large room decorated in yellows, oranges and reds, lots and lots of reds. A waist-high, slug-like thing with floppy ears and white cuffs on its tiny T-Rex arms oozes toward me.

"We expect you to be in the interview chamber at your appointed time, not in the vestibule." Its voice is a loud, deep baritone.

It must be a Napoleon, but that booming voice seems so out of place for something so small.

I bow low so that we see eye to eye and extend my hand. I don't know what else to do when greeting a sentient species. The ears look like they were put on by Salvador Dali; they just melt down the sides of his face. When he talks, his mouth-like thing opens and closes both up and down and side to side. At rest, it forms a plus sign. Now that I'm down this low, I can see a red bowtie beneath his double chin.

He takes my hand and I realize his cuffs are white silk with shiny gold cufflinks. It's the only clothing he's wearing. His whole body is covered in a layer of fat, so much so that I can't tell if he has feet.

"Before you can be introduced to the others, you must fill out the new interviewee form. It is required. Your predecessor Tim Wolff made it for us." He looks at me with big, sad eyes.

The blob's stubby little arm extends toward a darkened screen on my left. As I approach, it lights up. At the top is "Id10t Form." I scan the room with a half-smile. No one is smiling back.

In the far corner is a Yeti. It's splayed out, covering a maroon, four-seat couch all by itself. It nods at me. I glance away, so it doesn't think I'm staring. The creature has coarse white fur and three deadly black claws on each hand. Even lying down, I'd not want to get close to it. Its white furry head looks like it belongs on a cow-sized dog. I take a quick look at the face again and its sunken black eyes—straight out of a horror film—are staring back at me. There is very little information on the Yetis, and I understand why. Who would attempt to question them?

The Bwetnib I met in the hallway is flitting in circles while chattering to himself. High-pitched yelps and whines emanate from him, which in context makes me think he's happy. His head is much too big for his body, and the tusks rising from his lower jaw. They really do look like they came off a saber-toothed tiger.

On the opposite side of the room is an Erati. Most of the aliens have simple clothing, but not the Erati. She's—I think it's a she—is elaborately dressed. She's wearing a thick burgundy coat of down, I think, although it might be fur. But most striking is the sheer amount of jewelry she's wearing. There are four gold necklaces of various lengths, covering her entire chest. More golden bands zigzag along her forearms as well. She must have a hundred thousand dollars on display.

She locks eyes with me, so I lower my gaze and look for the last occupant in the room. The Umbran is nowhere to be seen.

"Ignore Calliope, she only babbles about her baubles," the wall beside me says. I do a double take as the vague outline moves away from the wall. The Umbra's camouflaging is even better than described. I hadn't noticed it until it spoke.

The Umbran draws in close and I get a whiff of his breath. My eyes start to water so I shield my face with my hands, then slowly lower them as I turn away from him. How can anything smell so fetid and still be living?

"Until it signs the form, it should ignore all of you," the officious slug says.

I scribble my name at the bottom of the screen and nod to the Napoleon.

"Welcome Scholar Anthony, wiseman of your kind and philosopher of anthropology, you will find hospitable your desk." His stubby arm points to a school desk along the wall near the Yeti. It's literally a high school desk with an opening for books underneath the writing surface.

I approach it cautiously, not looking at the Yeti. I take a seat and run my hand inside the opening, in case Tim left me any messages.

"My name is not pronounceable by your vibrating air chords. My human given name is Crighton. Tim bestowed upon me this exalted name."

"It is nice to meet you, Crighton."

The Bwetnib rushes over and hugs my knees, tight enough that I'm not sure I can break free. "I'mcalledBuddy," he says. "Canwebe good friends? We'llbegreat friends. BuddyandAnthony, that's us."

"Yes, we can be friends, Buddy. Did Tim give you that name also?" The first several words it speaks all tumble out at once. I can't help but wonder what would happen if it drank an energy drink. It might explode.

"Ooooohhhhhyouare very smart, just like Tim. ItoldTim all about my parade mates. Letmetell you about my parade mates. Theyarethe best."

"Is that what you call everyone gathered here?"

"Eww!" Buddy's face looks comically revolted. "Nothey'recolleagues. Igrewup on Bwetnib with my parade mates. Youcallmy planet Sirius c, but it is really called Bwetnib."

"Buddy," I interject, "I would like to meet the rest of our colleagues first, if you don't mind."

He seems a little disappointed. He takes two steps before diving into a head roll toward the Yeti. "Hernameis Grendel."

"We meet," she says. I wait for more, but that's it. After an awkward silence, I bow my head.

"It's good to meet you, Grendel." She mirrors my head nod.

Buddy walk-tumbles over to the Umbran, but he misjudges the distance and runs into it. The Umbra kicks him and poor Buddy goes careening across the room.

"I am called Shadow," it says. "I am the male of my species."

"My name is Anthony and I am also the male of my species."

Crighton huffs. "We are cognizant of your intimate constitution. The odor can hardly be mistaken."

"Ahh, thanks for letting me know?" I look around the room, but no one is willing to explain.

Shadow places both hands on my shoulders and draws his face uncomfortably close to mine. We are nearly the same height, so I turn my head so I don't receive another direct blast of putridity.

"How tall are you, Anthony?"

"I am six feet tall."

"That is the average for your species, yes? You do not deviate. We do not like deviants."

"Ahh, that means something slightly different, and not really pleasant, in my world." I get a blast of his breath, despite my efforts. Pepper spray isn't this nauseating. "Please forgive me, but there is one more colleague I need to meet." I forcibly lift his hands off my shoulders and take a step away.

"There is no need. Calliope will only bore you," he says.

The Erati is pressing her head against the glass of the one and only window, looking pensively at the stars. Her posture is one that every man should know; her feelings are hurt. As I get closer, her coat is neither fur nor feathers, but something in between.

"It is a pleasure to meet you, Calliope. I am Anthony." Once more, I bow.

"Calliope is I, you see

Pleasure meeting thee."

I blink my eyes a couple of times. Do they really speak in couplets? I thought that was a joke.

"Ahh, From Earth I come and rejoice, at being greeted by your voice."

A big smile erupts from her face. She makes sure that Shadow can see it. Within her mouth are at least a hundred sharp teeth. She grabs my hand possessively. She gives a purring noise and I'm all kinds of uncomfortable.

"How do all of you speak English so well?"

Grendel taps the side of her head, just under the ear. "Implants."

I wait for more, but that's all I get.

Shadow walks over, eyeing Calliope. "The implants translate your planet's native tongue directly to our speech centers. We answer in our own language, but the embedded micro speakers translate to your language."

"English is not exactly the official language of my planet, but it is very popular," I say. "But why don't I hear your language when you speak?"

"Noise cancellation," Shadow says, amused at my confusion.

"The tablet at your desk has the official bylaws of the observation program that you will need to learn thoroughly." Crighton says as he reasserts himself. He struggles to adjust his bowtie with his adorably tiny arms.

"Let me," I say. From one knee, I pull the bowtie out from under a roll of fat and stuff his second flabby chin underneath the tie. "There, now you look like the notable Napoleon you undoubtably are."

He bobs up and down a few times, which I assume means he's happy.

"Unfortunately, the others will not back my call for compulsory quizzes." His head turns two hundred and seventy degrees, like an owl's head would, except in his case, his quick movements cause his ears to splay out as he turns. Or maybe it's the low gravity. I'm not a physicist.

Staring at me with his sad little face, it's more comical than serious. A laugh escapes me and I'm forced to cover it up with a cough.

Shadow closes in on me again, but I can't take another blast of his breath. He rests his hand on my shoulder and attempts to match my skin tone, but it's too reddish. "Do you have a female mating partner?"

Calliope jumps from her perch and starts twiddling her highly decorated arms.

"Stop showing scarlet

You filthy harlot."

"I do, in fact, have a girlfriend." I remove Shadow's hand and step back, avoiding his attempted hug. He's much too familiar with strangers.

Do I? I haven't been able to talk to her since my abduction after my Ph.D. defense.

"If you have mate bonded, then you must shun further competition. It is the way," Shadow says, disappointed. "This is unfortunate, as it makes you uninteresting to me."

Before I can think, I raise a single finger up toward the Umbran. The gesture could be offensive to his people. I make a fist, so I'm not pointing at him or anyone else. "It is not unusual for my people to engage in physical competitions for the joy of doing so, not solely for acquiring a mate."

"Then we shall hunt mushmahhus together," Shadow says.

"What's a mushmahhu?" I ask, only slightly unnerved.

"It is cylindrical and long as a Yeti, with thousands of hollow needle hairs for stealing fluids from its prey," the Napoleon says with what I believe is a four-lipped smirk. "Your skin is soft, so it be drawn to you."

My stomach drops and I feel faint.

"Oh, look at the pretty colors." Shadow's face starts rippling various shades of white as well. "Is that how you attract a mate?"

When did this start going so very wrong?

"This," I wave my hand at my face, "is a sign of discomfort or sudden surprise in my species. Is there someplace we can go patrol? I'd love to learn more about the station."

"Tell us of your hunting exploits," Shadow says.

"I'm not a hunter," I say. "I've been busy studying for many years."

"Shadow's fortunes headed down

With sorrow, he will surely drown."

"Every human is proficient with weapons," Shadow says.

"I don't know who told you that . . .."

"Timdidand Tim never lies. He told us so," Buddy says.

"Well . . . there are different techniques and not all–"

A squealing pig noise blasts over the speaker, cutting me off. There are any number of squeaks and whines before the algorithm is able to decipher the cacophony.

"HelpI'mtrapped and all alone! Youmusthelp me now! Itisdark. Icannotsee."

Crighton slams the mute button. "This creature is not complying with the current communique code." He taps on the console. "It's coming from the Umbran ring." He looks accusingly at Shadow.

No one moves from their spot.

"We have to try to help this Bwetnib," I say. Tim did say to get everyone to patrol.

"I vote no," Shadow says peevishly.

"Concurring is Crighton."

"Wemusthelp him," Buddy says.

"The path forward there is no doubt

Helping sentients is what we're about."

Everyone focuses on me. I look at Grendel. She stares back impassively.

"Grendel, do you wish to speak?" I ask.

"No."

Everyone looks at me again. "Well, I'm going out there to look for this poor Bwetnib."

"You vote yay?" Crighton asks.

"Yes."

He looks disgusted at me and waddles for the door. Everyone else follows. With three great strides, Grendel catches up to me from the back of the room.

"Why didn't you vote?" I ask.

"Even numbers."

"But it was tied two to two. I don't understand."

"Correct." She walks past me, out the door and down the empty hallway.

As we get closer to the center of the ring, everyone starts skipping, then hopping, and finally floating to the lift as the gravity decreases.

The five of them wait for me in the lift. No one moves or says anything. They just stare at me as I float inside. I'm the only one not accustomed to transitioning from walking to floating.

"Um, does anyone know where we need to go?"

"Anthony's search," Grendel says unhelpfully.

"What floor should we go to first?"

"Only you can contact the buttons," Crighton says, the translation is loaded with his disdain.

"Because it's my search?"

"No," the little Napoleon says. "Buddy is not allowed, because he will not be able to get in his harness in time and the motion will cause him to run-tumble within the lift. Inevitably, he will collide with the button panel and us, making the trip intolerable."

I look at the others. Shadow and Calliope nod their heads in agreement. Crighton raises his tiny hand at the Bwetnib to shush him.

"Shadow doesn't want to be here, Grendel will never do so and Calliope's jewelry ends up hitting extra buttons."

"What level was the distress call on?" I ask.

"U7," the Napoleon harrumphs.

"What level are we on now?"

"C12. It is customary, though not yet a rule put forth by the council, to not linger in a lift for more than three seconds without selecting a destination," Crighton says in perfect bureaucratese.

"My bad." I glance at the panel. There are sixteen buttons, ten numbers, and the first six letters of the alphabet. "Um, what gives with the buttons?"

"Hexadecimal," the Yeti says.

"Um, I'm a little rusty on my hexadecimal." In truth, I only heard of it once, when my college roommate complained about his computer class.

Everyone remains still and I can feel my earlobes getting hot. If I don't do something fast, Shadow will think I'm flirting with him.

"Buddy!" I say with a little too much excitement.

"Yesgoodfriend Anthony?"

"Can you press the code for level U7, and only the buttons for U7?"

"OfcourseI can."

I turn to the Yeti. "Grendel, would you be willing and able to hold on to our esteemed Bwetnib, so he doesn't tumble during our trip?"

"Yes."

"Please, both of you, do so."

"Ooohhhh," Buddy says, as he pushes off much harder than necessary toward me. He's clapping vigorously and doesn't seem to notice that he's headed right at me. Fortunately, Grendel grabs him and redirects him to the panel.

Why do I feel like I've just promised to marry one of his parade mates?

Grendel

93

Age: Unknown

Sex: F

Species: Yeti

Social Status / Rank: Unknown

Height / Build: 10'10" (3.3 m)

Weight: 342 lbs (155.1 kg)

Hair color: White

Eyes color: Black

Marks/Tattoos: Unknown

Education / Training: Unknown

Skills/Talents: None demonstrated, low priority for technology

Chapter Six
Patrol

The lift opens on U7 and the lights on the ceiling activate. The heavy machinery makes the whole floor vibrate just a bit. There's a groaning noise coming from all around us.

"What's causing that noise?" I ask. I turn around to see everyone else staring at Crighton.

"I'll put in the proper paperwork for the repairs when we get back," he says with a frown on his face. At least, I think he's frowning. It's hard to tell.

"Ican'tsee! It'sdarkin here! Help! help! help!" There's a noise coming from down the hallway, but the voice comes from everyone's translator inserts.

Buddy the dynamo launches out of the elevator. As the gravity increases, he arcs toward the floor and switches to a run-tumble in one fluid motion. He rounds the corner without slowing. The rest of us look at each other, waiting for someone to act.

Shadow is the first to unbuckle his harness. "The damage done to my people's ring will be redressed." He pushes off to find the Bwetnibian missile.

"Do you wish to be carried?" Grendel asks.

I look up at her and realize she's not talking to me.

"No, though we won't stay long," Crighton says, giving me an irritated look.

Just as Shadow turns the corner, Buddy comes careening around him, crashing into the wall and halting the little creature's momentum.

"Ifoundhim!" he yells, faster and louder than normal. "Ifoundhim!"

Calliope keeps her hands against her chest, like she's afraid to touch anything. Crighton puffs and wheezes as the gravity gets more pronounced. Grendel walks with an amused look as we four bring up the rear.

"Hurry," Shadow says. "I do not wish to be seen here with all of you present."

Buddy takes the Umbran at his word and rolls back the way he came.

"We'recomingto get you!"

"Ican'tget out!"

The two Bwetnibs keep shouting the same words to one another, and it dead-eyed looks everyone is giving tell me they just want the shouting to end. I can't say that I disagree with them.

Crighton stops his waddling and leans against the corridor wall.

I wave the others forward toward the incessant noise while I hang back and wait with Crighton.

The Napoleon contorts his neck in all kinds of odd angles. He begins a clucking type noise, like he's trying to taste something that's burning his mouth. His head swivels until it's pointed directly behind him. He lowers his head as much as the double chins will allow. Before I can ask if he's alright, he gives a contented sigh.

"My species have pockets of various hormones stored throughout our bodies. By doing the appropriate motions, they are released. I will have increased strength in my legs for a time. Let's proceed."

"So you walk on legs?" I ask, then grimace. It's not my most artful conversation starter.

Thankfully, he ignores my question. "Has Tim informed you of my name's origin?" Crighton asks.

"He didn't have time."

"With my people, the k sound at the start of a name denotes immense respect. Since I am meticulous and undeniably right, I should be shown deference as the right one. His wisdom is undeniable. Tim is among the most astute your planet has to offer."

"Right one . . . Crighton," I say. "It makes sense."

"Obviously. It would be good that you remember this."

I have to look away so the little blob doesn't see me laughing. This is one case of the military getting it right. Crighton is as haughty as Napoleon ever was.

Buddy tumbles in circles in front of a laboratory door. Almost like he's doing egg rolls, but more chaotic. He's chanting "we'recoming" while a "helpme" is repeated over and over inside.

Shadow leans against the opposite wall looking at his claws while Calliope fans her face with her talons? Claws? Whatever they are. Grendel is looking at me with a subtle smile on her face. I try the door, but it's locked.

"That is against protocol," Crighton says. "See the Laboratory Standard Operating Procedure, section fourteen point three, paragraph six, line one." He imperiously waves his hand and the door opens. He turns to me and explains. "The door is not to be locked while a sentient is inside."

Does he think I did this or is he just uncomfortable with the increased gravity?

Buddy walks—actually walks—like a normal creature, past the chemical cabinets along the nearest wall toward the bench at the back of the lab. Each of the bottles has five different lines of scribbles written on the sign below it.

"What is this place?" I ask.

"Chemical storage

Free to forage."

Calliope smiles at my puzzlement.

"All of intellect

May freely select."

Someone is going to have to explain this to me. It can't be Buddy, Grendel hasn't made sense yet, and asking Shadow will only upset Calliope. "Crighton, can you explain what this place is?"

"As Calliope succinctly stated, this is a free laboratory for all intelligent species. Whatever your cleansing or health need may be, one comes here and formulates the appropriate mixture."

"So I can come in here and mix chemicals all willy-nilly?" I wonder how *that* will translate.

"All intelligent species," Crighton corrects me.

"So these five lines of scribbles?" I point to the nearest tag, though there is no chemical above it.

"Napoleonese is on top, of course. That particular compound is hydrolysate of natural oil, or as your people call it, sweet principle of fat, according to Carl Wilhelm Scheele in his treatise from 1783."

"Neither of those names mean anything to me." I'm regretting asking the little Napoleon.

"Glycerin is what it is called it their modern society," Shadow says over his shoulder.

"Modern?" Crighton asks. His mouth opens and closes up and down, then right and left, though no noise comes out.

"He laughs at your people," the Umbran says.

"That's how they laugh?" I ask. I squinch up my eyes. I'm not sure why, but I find it horrifying.

"Indeed," Grendel says, also smiling.

"Whatever, let's just free this guy before my fillings pop out," I say.

"Fillings?" Crighton asks. "Are these fillings in your intestinal tract?"

I walk away from the little slug. If I tell them about my dental problems, they'll all want to gaze at my teeth. Who knows, maybe that's how Tim got kissed by a Bwetnib.

The repeated calls are coming from behind a laboratory bench. I try, but I can't budge it. Shadow and Calliope are playing a game of 'who can look most unconcerned', so I motion to the Yeti for help.

Grendel goes down to her knees and reaches behind the bench. With one quick yank, the bench pulls away from the wall and the creature, um, species, is freed. Grendel stands up and holds the audible offender by the big, bushy tail. It's an auburn colored creature with the tusks and eyes of a Bwetnib, but with a pudgy body. Not as globby as a Napoleon, but it does have tiny T-Rex arms.

"Is that a Bwetnib or a Napoleon?" I ask.

Grendel drops the creature, and it runs in circles, though upright and much slower than our Buddy.

"What species are you?" I ask.

The creature looks at us, falls down, and curls its tail between its legs to cover its stomach.

"It is an abomination," Crighton says in an uber disapproving tone. "A blight upon my people."

The poor creature stares at us, befuddled.

"What parade group are you from?" Buddy asks.

The creature wails with a few clicks thrown in just for fun.

Buddy leans in closer and both voices are translated into English, thanks to Buddy's implant.

"I tried to escape from Murg, but he chased me here. I hid behind the counter, but he pushed it against the wall, trapping me."

Shadow pushes forward and looks down at our victim.

The creature freezes for a moment, then runs for the opening behind the lab bench. Grendel grabs its tail and hoists it up again.

"We're here to free you," I say. "Not to return you to . . . Murg."

The creature squirms even more.

"No implant," Grendel says.

"Let him go," I say.

Grendel drops him on his head.

"What is your name?" I ask, but it's no use. He can't understand me and I can't understand him.

The others remain staring in silence, except Crighton, who has turned his back and is growling to himself. "Acidum nitricum is missing too," he grumbles. "The wretched creature has made an explosive in its ignorance."

It makes a weird noise, like there are only vowels and no consonants in his language.

"I have no name," Buddy translates.

"Are you truly a hybrid between the Napoleons and the Bwetnibs?" I ask via Buddy.

"That is what Murg said."

I scratch my head. "Let's call you Dingo."

"Thatisgreat!" Buddy blurts out. "Dingo! Youtoohave Earthly sage given name." He grabs the strange creature and starts jumping up and down.

Soon, they're both doing it. It's against my anthropological training, but it's infectious, so I start jumping too. Crighton purses his four lips outward and flings his head away from me. His ears lift from his head and he looks like a helicopter with floppy rotors.

There's a deafening boom as the lab bench where Dingo was trapped lurches toward us and smolders. We're all knocked to the floor, even Grendel.

From where I was thrown, I can see a gaping hole behind the smoking bench. Calliope rushes to the hole and points downward.

"The criminal below

Looks like Shadow!"

"Don't believe her," Shadow says. "They always blame my kind."

"An Umbra I call

For that I saw."

"I blame the hybrid," Crighton says as she shivers. "He is . . . unnatural."

"It was Murg!" Dingo says. "He swore he would get me, if only in pieces."

"What did the Umbra look like?" I ask.

I get silent looks, and Buddy doesn't even try to translate.

"Oh, sorry, forgot about the camouflaging abilities." I can't help but feel stupid.

"Kidnapping, theft, intentional damage to the station, locking the chemical lab, misappropriation of chemicals, attempted violence," Crighton takes a breath. "Filling out the necessary forms will take hours."

"We can do that later," I say. "Let's apprehend the perp first."

"Paperwork can never be dismissed. It is the hallmark of intelligent species. Is not the Id10t form revered on your planet?" Crighton asks, shocked.

"Sure," I stretch out the word. "But we need to apprehend the saboteur."

"We must all return and fill out the requisite forms," Crighton says in an overly loud voice.

The others turn away.

"Crighton, you are the expert at this, and I am sure Dingo has not filed his notice of arrival on the station," I say.

"Exactly right!" The little slug says. "There is the arrival form, the undocumented fine," he looks at the scared little alien, "the poverty rider, the criminal report, the witness statement for the explosion and theft of–"

"Yes, there are many, many forms to fill out," I cut in. "And I bet you'll even come up with new ones as you walk Dingo back to our office."

Crighton's mouth opens up and down, then left and right. "You are right! I will be filling in forms for the rest of the shift," he says with excitement.

"Approved," Grendel says with a smirk.

The Napoleon is oblivious.

"He'll need a translator thingy," I say, "unless you want to take Buddy with you as well."

"It speaks Umbran," Crighton says. "All intelligent species have an implant."

"Is there a form for someone who doesn't possess an implant?" I ask. "An expert paper work maestro like you could probably devise a new form to capture these types of situations."

His mouth opens wide in both directions, showing me a throat full of teeth. "You are very wise; I did not think it is possible for you to contribute meaningfully."

"Thanks?"

Crighton turns to our scared little victim. "Come with me, Dingo, I will instruct you in the proper ways of the Napoleons."

"Isithard to be a Napoleon?" Crighton's implant captures the hybrid's excited talk and translates into English.

I'm going to have to ask how that works. Does everyone hear English?

"No talking," Crighton says. "I will recite my favorite forms from memory, as all good Napoleons do."

Poor Dingo, he walks with his head down, like a poor school kid being escorted to the principal's office. Perhaps he'll start tumbling at Crighton's side, but that most definitely would not be Napoleonic.

* * *

"Shall we go look for this Umbran?" I ask.

"Sniff for him, you mean?" Shadow says.

"Yes," Grendel says.

She lifts me up, until my legs dangle uselessly and walks toward the blast hole. She leans over and we both inspect the damage. The smoke and dust have mostly cleared, and only a rubble pile can be seen below. Without warning, she drops me and I land hard on one knee. I grimace as I pull a small metal shard out of my shin.

Can I get tetanus out here?

Shadow jumps down next, well clear of the jagged edges surrounding me. He extends a hand and I extract myself from the pile. Buddy lets out a high-pitched squeal as he leaps from above. Shadow catches him and hands him off to me in one fluid motion.

Calliope leaps next and falls into me. I stumble over Buddy and break my fall with the back of my head. As I get up, there's a stinging pain along with a dull ache. I touch the painful spot and my hand comes away red with blood. I lean forward, so the blood will roll off my forehead and not stain my shirt.

Shadow comes over and licks the cut. He cocks his head to one side and smiles as he blasts me with his putrid breath. My eyes water, so I turn away. There's a rubbery glue ball sticking to my skull and matting my hair. I draw my hand away, but the jellified saliva stays put. I tap it a couple of times. It's already hardened into a rubbery consistency.

"Thank you," I say, holding up my hand and creating space between us. "That should be enough."

Not satisfied, Shadow falls to his knees and licks my shin as well.

"Very tasty," he says.

I give him a frozen smile.

Nobody said anything about alien vampires.

"Lead," Grendel says.

"So . . . does anyone know which way he went?"

"Scent trail clear,

To all those near."

"Right," I say. "But not to me." I look over my choices.

"Calliope, I choose thee. Lead the way and do not stray."

That was terrible. I need to brush up on my poetry.

The Erati wiggles her lower jaw back and forth, making squishing noises. She takes the lead and walks with a determined air.

Shadow follows right behind Calliope, matching each step and almost touching her as she makes her way along the corridors.

"What is up with those two?" I ask Buddy and Grendel.

"Pheromones," the Yeti answers.

Tim said that no one can get the Yetis talking. "What is your world like, Grendel?"

"Round, wet and dry, warm and cold."

"Thank you," I respond without a touch of exasperation.

"Myworldis hilly and nice and sometimes wet, but I don't like the wet places," Buddy offers. "Werollthrough the forests and meadows, but not the beaches. Weavoidthe water."

"What is that?" I point to a punctured pipe hanging down from the ceiling.

"Carbon monoxide," Shadow says after tasting the air.

"If monoxide flies

The human dies."

"I don't smell anything."

The others shake their heads. Why?

"For scent use, humans obtuse," Grendel says.

The others start gibbering and howling in what I can only assume is laughter at my expense. Shadow's piercing high yelps are the exact opposite of what I would expect. Buddy is barking out laughter punctuated with yips as he tumbles haphazardly about the chamber.

"I can't stay here, guys. Carbon monoxide is toxic, even in small doses." I'm not sure about that, but hopefully it will spur them on to action. I wait for a response, but no one seems bothered but me.

"Before end is met, safety I must get. Concentration too high, we all will die." If I use couplets, maybe they'll listen to me.

"A doublet of couplets," Shadow says as he kicks at Buddy's pinballing form.

A red light starts flashing and the doors of the chamber seal. The others are . . . unconcerned.

"So can we fix it? Or do we call Crighton and have him deal with it?"

"He'd document with care; we'd run out of air." Even Buddy is getting in on the couplets now.

The others start laughing again.

"Solutions, people!" I brace myself against the wall, since my feet are unsteady.

Grendel pats me on the top of my head and nearly breaks my neck. She bites the pipe, creating two crimps in it. The gas is whistling now as it escapes. She bends each crimp ninety degrees and the whistling stops. "Proceed." She grabs me by the neck and steers be out of the chamber.

"Thank you for stopping the leak," I say.

"No hearing gas gripe, screeching from pipe?" Shadow asks.

"Nope."

"At what else is your species deficient?" He asks.

"Too many questions! We have a suspect to find," I say.

Buddy sniffs the air and run-tumbles into the lead. "The Umbran is up ahead!"

"Bwetnibs are unaffected by lack of oxygen?" I ask.

"Brain cells dead, in empty head," Grendel murmurs.

"Hereheis!" Buddy yells.

⟨ɾⲓ⟨ʒ⟩ꟼʏⲧⴲↄ

Age: Unknown

Sex: M

Species: Napoleon

Social Status / Rank: Presumed high (unknown social structure)

Height / Build: 2'10" (86.4 cm)

Weight: 80 lbs (36.3 kg)

Hair color: Brown, White

Eyes color: Brown

Marks/Tattoos: Wears bowtie and cuffs

Education / Training: Unknown

Skills/Talents: Legalistic/Bureaucratic – avoid if possible

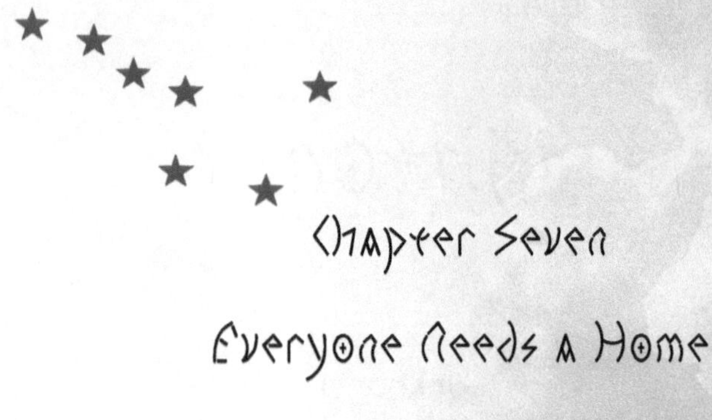

Chapter Seven

Everyone Needs a Home

The Umbran villain, Murg, leans against the wall next to the elevators. His skin perfectly mimics the steel gray panel behind him, except for his whitish face. His dark brown eyes look over our group before settling on me.

"You have one of the new pets," it says.

"Youareunder arrest for kidnapping," Buddy says. The little Bwetnib stands right below our perp and waggles his fingers.

The Umbran kicks Buddy hard in the chest, causing him to tumble into the opposite lift. Shadow hits the up button and the doors start closing. Buddy run-tumbles out from the closing doors and emits a threatening growl. He lunges at Murg, but Grendel grabs the Bwetnib by the scruff of the neck in mid-jump and holds him aloft.

"What species did I kidnap?" The smiling older Umbran asks.

"YoukidnappedDingo!" Buddy yells while gesticulating wildly.

Grendel raises her eyebrows—such a human gesture—and gives a subtle smile at the feisty little Bwetnib.

"You'recomingwith us," Buddy announces.

"Only five species

Protected by *dæcrees*."

"He'scomingwith us!" Buddy says while still kicking feet in the air. "Crighton will find a crime."

The elder Umbra takes a couple of threatening steps until Grendel points at the Umbran. "Come."

The Umbra looks up at Grendel before looking for support within our group. Shadow is unwilling to meet his gaze, while Calliope and I glare at him.

"I am Murg, and come I will."

We make it to the lift without incident, thanks to Grendel's imposing demeanor. Buddy hits the button and we wait in silence.

Longest elevator ride ever.

* * *

Crighton lets out a fart-like noise from his double mouth when he sees us. His ears flop as he jumps from the chair. His big, sad eyes settle on me for the explanation.

"Wecaughtthe criminal!" Buddy blurts. Grendel grabs the top of his head before he can start running in circles.

"I want my property back," the Umbran says.

Grendel chuckles, for unfathomable reasons.

"You brought this . . . abomination, onto the station?" Crighton asks with a glimmer in his eyes. "There will be an illegal entry fine, an air waiver fee, recycling fines and illegal transportation of a dangerous creature penalty." Crighton looks more animated now than ever. "Those are just the beginning. There's an emergency housing fine, and a belated meal ticket fee, which is no longer eligible for the new arrival discount."

His little cuffs look like they might fly off his arms with his attempt at expansive movements. Unfortunately, his teeny arms make it an impossibility. Still, it's the most animated I've ever seen the little Napoleon.

"He wasn't brought onto the station by me or anyone," Murg says.

Crighton taps the console. "Other than who-mans, there are no inferior species registered."

"Hey!" I say. "That's insulting to both Dingo and me."

"If inferior be,

Insults recede."

"Who's side are you on?" I ask Calliope.

"Spacefaring able?

Equal a fable."

I block Calliope's face from view with my hand. "In any case, we caught the criminal who kidnapped Dingo."

"No one's been kidnapped, and no one's been brought on this station against their will," a smirking Murg says. He must have an implant as well.

"Then how did he get here?" I ask.

"Bred here."

Poor Crighton's head nearly explodes. The bottom half of his mouth falls without a trace of noise coming from it.

"Just ask the commandant of the station," Murg says. "The Napoleons knew."

"True," Grendel says.

"What?" Buddy and Crighton yell in unison.

"Project hidden, because forbidden," Grendel says.

I don't know if I can handle everyone speaking in rhymes.

Crighton's slug form blanches. "We'll discuss this another time. Leave us, *Umbran filth.*"

"With my property?" Murg goads the little slug.

"You can't afford the fines," Crighton says, his voice quivering. He hits a button and a screen behind the offending Umbran lights up. "Sign there to abandon your property, or else you'll have to mortgage the Umbran disk to pay off all the fines."

Murg gives the barest hint of a smile as he rests his hand on the console. The screen brightens for a second, then goes dark. He cocks his head sideways before turning for the door. "I can always engineer more," he says over his shoulder.

Before Buddy can go ballistic, Grendel rests her hand on the top of his head. "More to story."

No one seems willing to share their thoughts in the presence of Murg, so we watch in silence as he leaves. There's a collective exhale once the door closes.

Maybe it's because of the dachshunds earlier, but I scratch Dingo behind the ears. He turns his head into my fingers and the tension in the little guy melts away.

"Dingo is not a member of one of the five signatory species of this station." Crighton refuses to look in Buddy's direction, so he fixates on me instead. "Or a protected lesser species," he motions to me. "Therefore, Murg the Umbran is correct in his assertion that he cannot be prosecuted in this locality."

The Bwetnib goes to our poor orphan and starts sniffing him.

"Whataboutme?" Dingo asks. Thanks to Buddy's uncomfortably close proximity, I can understand the hybrid.

"We can't just let Dingo go! That Umbran will just rekidnap him," I say.

"There is no statute against it," Crighton says, but without his regular gusto. "Unless the Bwetnibs claim him as one of their own?" Crighton asks.

"Theparadecouncil must decide," Buddy says. "Buttheyare on holiday down on the planet."

"Can you contact them?" I ask.

"No."

Poor Buddy, his head sinks down to the point that he almost falls over. "They will not be back until the Interspecies Council convenes."

"None of my kind will accept him," Crighton says.

"Nowhere to belong

Such a sad song."

"He can join the human contingent," I blurt out, "if he so chooses."

Crighton frowns at me. "Most unusual." He goes back to tapping on his pad. "The topic of species expansion for probational species is not dealt with in the station's charter." He taps some more. "It will be added as unresolved issue two hundred and thirty-seven and added to the docket in . . . four point seven standard years. Assuming that you have the capacity to speak for your species on this topic."

"Nowhere is it written that I don't," I respond with a touch of defiance.

Everyone looks at me, doubtful.

"My aunt is Colonel Katie Janeway, and by familial extension, I speak for her on this matter, unless or until she countermands my claim."

Buddy and Dingo start jumping up and down, which, of course, leads to them tumbling erratically about the office.

Tim told me not to mention having a girlfriend, which I did. He told me not to mention the familiar relationship with Aunt Katie, which I just did. Could this be more of a disaster?

"As for Dingo, provisionally of the who-man contingent, your presence here is against station policy and you must leave the station or fill out the requisite forms."

"Where will I find them?" Dingo asks, hugging Buddy so he can be understood.

Crighton points to a data terminal. "Until you have completed all the forms properly, you are a non-entity and will be treated as livestock."

Dingo's four bug eyes get even larger as his expression falls. If he were human, the tears would be starting.

"That's a bit harsh, Crighton. Dare I say that it is not the correct way to handle the situation?"

The outraged blob bounces up and down, sending rippling waves of fat vertically along his body. "There is proper protocol for a reason. It is not to be dismissed when inconvenient. That is what separates us from lesser, planet-bound intelligences." His mouth quivers side to side and one foot emerges from his fat roll, displaying four inch long claws.

The others crowd around, sensing a spectacle, no doubt.

I press my palms together. "Forgive me, I spoke in haste and with frustration. I only meant that from my experiences, compassion will yield much the same result and will not scar the recipient, who is a blameless victim in this case." I keep my voice firm, knowing I'm in the right.

Crighton's foot retracts, and he lowers himself an inch from his full, *menacing* height back to his regular stature. "Your opinion has been noted," he says frostily.

"WhatdoI do after I'm finished?" Dingo asks, shaken by the whole ordeal.

"We have no unassigned quarters in the who-man area, so talk to your species mate about sharing his quarters." Crighton's droopy ears raise slightly and he displays slightly upturned lips.

Is he smirking at me?

* * *

I watch the seconds count down on my watch. My first shift is almost over and, well, at least I didn't get all of us *who-mans* kicked off the station. There's a lot to unpack from the aliens, but I'm getting a handle on the males, Shadow, Crighton and Buddy. Calliope and Grendel are still mysterious though.

"I have filed a motion of protest against the inclusion of the creature Dingo to the human contingent," Crighton says.

"That is not necessary," I say. "We have found an amicable solution that keeps Dingo safe from Murg and is not a burden upon your clade." Glancing over, Dingo is mercifully oblivious to our discussion. He's propping his head up with his left hand as he fights his way through the forms.

Bored with the whole ordeal, Calliope has retreated to the sofa. Shadow and Grendel absently kick Buddy back and forth. If I could only get this slug to cut me a break.

"How about you claim Dingo for your people and I'll rescind my claim?" I say to Crighton.

"No, he cannot join my clade."

"Then why are you protesting?" I ask, exasperated.

"To withhold final determination until the Alternating Monthly Inter Species Assembly. The next meeting will be in twenty-three days."

"It will be decided then?" I ask.

"No, it will be listed as a topic of discussion. The AMISA agenda is already set for the next interstellar year and has multiple high value issues yet to be scheduled."

"And what about me? Will I be sent back to Earth six hours after I've arrived?"

"That is for your elder, aunt, Lieutenant Colonel Katie Janeway, to determine," Crighton says.

"Please call her Colonel Janeway. It would be best if my family connection to her doesn't become common knowledge."

"Secret?" Grendel asks, suddenly interested. "Silence price?" She and Shadow stop kicking Buddy.

Within seconds, I'm surrounded, and more than a little uncomfortable. "Look, I just got here and have no money, no possessions." I let out a single grunt. "I don't even have my own quarters anymore."

I glance at Dingo, but he's transfixed by the screen in front of him.

Crighton talks over everyone else. "All must be compensated for this secret to be kept."

"Hemustsee my people first!" Buddy shouts. "Theyareplanetside and must know of Dingo."

"Each a meeting," Grendel says.

"Five trips a must

To seal our trust."

Calliope and Shadow are both smiling.

I pull at the neck of my shirt. It's become quite warm in here.

"Agreed," I say.

"Hewillmeet my parade mates first!" Buddy shouts in triumph.

"He must join me in the gladiatorial games," Shadow says.

"His presence fills us

At feast of Gillus."

I spin around and look at Grendel. She smiles back, but says nothing.

"What about you, Crighton?"

"I need to inspect the who-man base where he," the slug points toward Buddy, "landed on your world."

"You mean an audit? You want to audit the base?"

"I am unfamiliar with this word, audit," Crighton says.

"It means you go to the base and inspect all the records to make sure that the humans have procedures and that they are properly following—and documenting—them in a meticulous manner."

Crighton's horizontal mouth parts turn upwards, into a smile. Then the vertical lips flatten out so his smile can reach clown-like proportions. It is oh, so creepy.

"Metoome too!" Dingo yells. Somehow he escaped everyone's notice as they were forcing concessions from me and joined the circle of Inquisitors. "Ineedto see my new homeworld if I'm to keep the secret."

"If I'm going to do this for all of you, then I want an implant so that I can understand what is going on around me," I say.

"Ineedone too!" Dingo yells.

I cover my ears in annoyance. Great, and he's my roommate.

"Hole in the head, hope you not dead," Grendel says with a wry smile, or indigestion, I'm not sure.

Crighton taps his panel a few more times. "The forms have been delivered to your Aunt . . . to Colonel Janeway. Please ensure they are filled out promptly and correctly."

Oh joy. And I was worried about the aliens. It's my people that will kill me first.

S)1a⏁ow

Age:	Unknown
Sex:	M
Species:	Umbran
Social Status / Rank:	High (Unknown social structure)
Height / Build:	6'0" (1.82 m)
Weight:	185 lbs (83.9 kg)
Hair color:	Brown, White
Eyes color:	Brown
Marks/Tattoos:	Wears neckerchief
Education / Training:	Unknown
Skills/Talents:	Athletic, primary target for technology

Chapter Eight
Family Reunion

Finally, there's adequate lighting, so the white enamel walls and door look white instead of dim and brooding. My anticipation of scorn and ridicule is already dark enough. The too small, crooked Space Force seal is a source of embarrassment to me now that I'm surrounded by five advanced races. What must they think of us? We can't even affix a label properly.

The empty corridor does nothing for the human contingent, either. Couldn't they at least get some houseplants or pictures of Earth's natural beauty? Anything to draw the eye away from the sorry sign would be an improvement. Despite my training, I'm beginning to think of these guys as my friends. Maybe that's crazy and they're just too different from us, but I don't think so. I can feel the connection.

"Bright." Grendel says.

"Too bright, but deficient are who-man eyes," Crighton says.

I give the little slug an irritated look. "I don't know the code to open the doors," I say.

Crighton heads straight for the touchpad and waves his hand over it. The doors open, much to the surprise of me and the slouching human guard inside.

He jumps to his feet and holds his hands out like he's going to stop us all from charging.

"An urgent matter for Colonel Katie Janeway, concerning Anthony the anthropologist, has arisen," Crighton says. He points at me as if picking out the human from this crowd isn't obvious.

"You can't go past this point without an escort," the guard says nervously. "Stay here." He turns and doesn't exactly run, but he moves faster than decorum would dictate.

Crighton starts to follow the guard, but I gently place my hand on his. Well where a shoulder would be on a human. Crighton's skin just pushes in, like there's gelatin inside. I squeeze a little and the skin turns rock hard.

What would Dr. Ben say? Do I really need a reminder that these are not humans?

Crighton looks up at me with his four lips extended to a point.

"Oh, I'm sorry," I remove my hand, "this gesture is common on Earth. It signifies to wait just a moment. I meant no offense."

His mouth relaxes and I wonder how close I came to an interspecies incident. There haven't been enough disasters added to today's tally. I'm pretty sure I'm the new record holder with or without this dust up.

"What is the urgent matter?" The booming voice of Aunt Katie precedes her into the foyer.

Dad always said that Aunt Katie never speaks to anyone, she only shouts.

"Colonel Katie Janeway," Crighton says, every bit as assertive, "this who-man," he unnecessarily points to me once again, "claims to be of the same lineage as you and claims that by said bond, he is able to speak for you on matters when you are not available."

Aunt Katie takes in the whole motley crew, but says nothing. I had nuns for all twelve years of Catholic school, and even taking the worst of all of them and merging them together, they would still be less imposing than Aunt Katie.

"Furthermore," Crighton continues unperturbed, "he has agreed to accept this unrecognized creature under the charter of who-mankind." His short hand waves vaguely toward Dingo and Buddy and Calliope.

I open my mouth to explain, but I have no idea where to start. Instead, I open and close it like a fish out of water. Aunt Katie's dead eyes rest on me while she nods her head slightly.

"Where is this creature?" She asks.

"Dingoisstanding right here, next to me," Buddy shouts before falling to the floor and doing his modified eggroll circles.

Dingo bounces up and down as his arms wave energetically. His Napoleon inherited fat rolls ripple up and down in waves from his knees to his shoulders.

Aunt Katie says nothing while she eyes each and every one of us. "Please, y'all, do come with me to our meeting room. This is a great honor for a distinguished representative of all the station's original species to join us here."

Huh? I've known Aunt Katie for all of my twenty-seven years and I have never heard her talk like a southern belle hosting a party.

We file into the meeting room and see Tim seated there, hurriedly pulling a credit card like thing from aunt Katie's laptop. The large screen says it can't find the video source. He gets up and turns the screen off for good measure.

The meeting table is just two foldout tables like you'd find in a school lunchroom. They haven't even put a tablecloth over it. The only things they added were rubber feet, so they don't move easily on the white metal floor.

"Do sit down," Aunt Katie says.

Crighton and Dingo remain standing, since they can't jump up into seats. Grendel sits on the corner of the table, since she's way too big to fit in a human chair. Tim nods his head at everyone.

"Crighton, can you explain what brings you and your colleagues here?" Aunt Katie asks.

"There are two overriding matters with several subpoints," the meticulous Napoleon says. "First, Anthony has stated that by familial connection to you, he speaks for you unless or until you deem it otherwise."

"I see." Aunt Katie's flinty gray eyes bore into me.

I have to look away. The room is quiet, so I look up and see everyone staring at me.

"Oh, sorry!"

Please face, don't turn red.

"Dingo here was rescued from his captor while we were on patrol," I say.

"Murgisa bad, bad Umbran!" Buddy shouts.

"Since he is a genetic hybrid between Bwetnibs and Napoleons, he belongs to neither."

Buddy nods energetically. It's only a matter of time before he starts rolling again.

"He was going to be turned out and likely be recaptured by an Umbran named Murg." The neck on my shirt feels tight, but I force myself not to tug at it. Mom told me that was one of my many tells when I was a kid. "So, speaking for you, I offered to accept Dingo into the human contingent to save him from slavery." I look up and meet Aunt Katie's eyes.

"What else?" she says. "The esteemed Napoleon said there were two main points.

Crighton puffs up at the flattery. That will be useful later, if I'm not kicked off the station the same day I arrive.

"The second issue," I grimace and look toward Tim's unforgiving eyes. "Well, it involves . . . an agreement . . .."

"Crighton," Aunt Katie says with agitation, "can you describe the second issue?"

"Anthony told us that you and he are kin, then later asked that we keep that information confidential. We have agreed to do so, pending the completion of certain conditions."

Aunt Katie's eyes flit to me before resting on Tim. "What are the conditions?"

"Anthony, your kin by way of your brother, his father, has agreed to attend an event from each of us at a time and place of our choosing. Furthermore, to facilitate these trips, Anthony has requested a translation insert be surgically installed into his and Dingo's heads."

"I see," Aunt Katie says, drawing out the final syllable. "With the understanding that, at the earliest possible interval, you will confirm Anthony's proclamations with me, he can speak for me." She looks right through me. "But as the commander of the human contingent here, I am available at all hours, so the necessity of Anthony making command decisions should be nil."

She walks over to Dingo and extends her hand. "Welcome Dingo, we would love to have you become one of us. Is that what you want?"

Buddy translates, causing Dingo to grab her hand and bounce up and down a few times before falling to the floor. He attempts to do the Bwetnib eggroll, but mostly he just rocks back and forth while his poofy tail hits the floor.

Aunt Katie smiles indulgently and walks back over to Tim. "As our security officer, what do you think of these one-on-one undertakings and the translation insert for Anthony?"

Tim stands up and jerks on his jumpsuit, straightening out the wrinkles. "I think for better understanding, these trips are essential." As an afterthought, he adds, "assuming our colleagues can ensure his safety."

"In the gladiatorial games, one must look to their own safety," Shadow says, stepping forward.

"Agreed."

Apparently, my safety isn't *that* important to our security officer. "As for the insert, will you leave it with us so that our doctor can perform the operation?"

"No," Crighton says. "Your people have no understanding of the device. However, your surgeon will be allowed to attend and advise during the procedure."

"Colonel Janeway was a nurse before entering the military," Tim says. "Both as a comfort to Anthony and because she has the necessary skills, we would request that she attends the procedure."

Aunt Katie nods.

It's weird inside my head right now. I know I should be worried about a surgery performed by, well, I don't even know what race will install the tech that no human understands, but all I can think of is how cool it will be to understand everything they say. I mean, these species are way more advanced than us, so it has to be routine, I hope.

"Is there anything else?" Aunt Katie asks. No one speaks up. "In that case, Anthony, Tim and I have a previously scheduled meeting we must attend. Thank you all for this great honor." Aunt Katie inclines her head.

"One should never be late to meetings!" Crighton says emphatically. He waves his arms in an attempt to shoo the others out of the room. At least, that's my best guess. For all I know, he could be releasing more hormones into his bloodstream.

Tim is up and out of his seat at once. He steers me by the elbow out of the room before any of the other species even leave. That seems a little rude to me, but Tim doesn't care. He takes me down the short hallway, turns left and opens the first door he sees.

Two women look up from another couple of lunchroom tables pushed together.

Seriously? This is the best they could get?

"The colonel and I need this room immediately for a debrief," Tim says.

The women immediately close their laptops and pack up their belongings. "Sir," the blonde says, "these two dogs were sent from Earth for the colonel."

"I'll see that she gets them," Tim says.

So that's why they were brought up. Who knew Aunt Katie had a soft spot for anything?

⟨ΛＬＬＩＯ⟩Ｅ

Age:	Unknown
Sex:	F
Species:	Erati
Social Status / Rank:	Unknown
Height / Build:	5'11" (86.4 cm)
Weight:	191 lbs (86.6 kg)
Hair color:	White, brown
Eyes color:	Brown
Marks/Tattoos:	Wears brown coat, always
Education / Training:	Unknown
Skills/Talents:	Astronomer, lesser target for technology

Chapter Nine

Debrief

Tim closes the door and runs a handheld device over my entire body.

"You're clean, have a seat."

The room is a bright white, with enamel or something covering the walls, floor and ceiling.

"Do you not have the budget to hang a picture or even a calendar?" I ask.

"This alloy is incredibly strong," Tim replies. "Drill bits just shatter if we try to put a hole in them." He kicks his feet up on the table and leans back in his chair. "Now, about your first day, I didn't think you could navigate yourself out of a wet paper bag, so you cleared that very low bar."

"It was thanks to you preparing me so well," I reply.

The door opens and Aunt Katie frowns at Tim. Reluctantly, he drops his feet to the floor. Dingo squeezes in between Aunt Katie and the door before she can shut it. He ducks under her arm and rushes over to me.

She takes the chair at the head of the table and rests her palms on it. She looks at Dingo, then me, then back to the newest addition to the human contingent again. The dachshunds pick this time to start barking and twirling inside their cage.

"What are they doing here?" Aunt Katie points at the dogs.

Dingo waddles over to the crate and lays down in front of it. He starts talking in Umbran to the dogs.

"The dachshunds are a present from General Poppy," Tim says with a smirk.

Aunt Katie starts to speak, then thinks better of it. "We have more important issues." She looks at Dingo, still laying on the floor.

"What are we to do with him?"

Dingo turns and faces us, somehow guessing that he's the topic of conversation. Unfortunately, none of us understand him or him us.

"Crighton suggested there are no spare human rooms, so he has to bunk with me."

Aunt Katie stops herself from speaking and takes a deep breath instead. "Dingo, can you find your way back to the other aliens?"

He looks at us, uncomprehending.

"Dingo," I say. "Buddy?"

The little guy stands up and attempts to say Buddy in his tongue.

I point at the door. "Buddy!"

Dingo wiggles his fingers at the puppies and they go crazy again. They jump up and lean into the crate door, getting their bodies nearly vertical. The hybrid scratches the smooth-haired dachshund's chest, but only for an instant. The long-haired one will have none of that. He, well, clearly they're both male, jumps into the reasonable puppy and knocks him down. Each time Dingo goes to pet the long-haired dachshund, it tries to bite him.

"Let him leave with those two as well," my aunt says.

"Really?" I ask. "What if they get hopelessly lost?"

"With the amount of noise they're making? Not likely," Tim says.

"I'm allergic, and one way or another, they will remain far away from me," Aunt Katie says.

I open the crate and the wiener dogs give me a quick sniff, but they are fascinated with Dingo and won't leave his diminutive side.

Aunt Katie opens the door. "Go on," she shouts. "Anthony won't be long."

Because as we all know, if someone doesn't understand you, shouting makes it better.

The door closes and my aunt shakes her head.

"We have enough problems already," Aunt Katie says. "What are we supposed to do, build a dog park?"

The spook tries to act consoling, but he's as fake as a three-dollar bill, to borrow a saying from Dad.

"I'm sorry to create such a commotion, Aunt Katie."

She gives me a disappointed look. "First, you will refer to me as Colonel Janeway or as ma'am from now on." She stares at me.

"Yes, ma'am."

"Good. Second, you will not speak for me ever again. If you try to do so, I will have you shipped back to Earth on the next available transport."

"How often are they?" I ask.

"You will speak only when a commanding officer gives you leave," Tim says.

"You're not a commanding officer," I say, leaning across the table.

"The cub gets a sociology degree and thinks that makes him something," Tim says.

"Sociology deals with societies. Anthropology deals with cultures. Spooks spread mistrust wherever they go. Why do you think they opened up to me so fast?"

"Listen here you little runt–"

"Stop it! Both of you." Aunt Katie rises from her seat. "Either whip 'em out and see whose is bigger or else act civil."

"Sorry, Kat," Tim mutters as he sits back down.

"Do you have pet names for each other?" I ask, disgusted.

"That's none of your business," Tim says in his best macho tone of voice.

"What does she call you? Timberwolf?"

Aunt Katie's face goes pale and Tim's flushes red.

"You will be very careful about what you say to the aliens and everyone else on this station," Aunt Katie growls.

"I didn't ask to get shanghaied," I tell my aunt. "And I'm not one of your little toadies." I point at Tim.

Aunt Katie stands up. "I am in charge of all the humans here," she pauses before continuing in a low voice. "If you want to stay and ultimately win a Nobel Prize for your pioneering work with alien races, then you will learn deference to the chain of command. Do you understand?"

I take a deep breath through my nose. Mom always says that it calms you down. "I will take my leave then, and return to the aliens, who don't act combative to justify their status. And you two will have the room all to yourselves." I head toward the door. There's no light switch, otherwise I'd turn the lights out for them.

"You will get your act together or you will be booted off this place," Aunt Katie says.

I open the door before I turn back to them. "General Alexanders told us all before we left that only the best should be here. If we see anyone falling below that standard, anyone at all, we are to inform her at once, though I'm not sure when I'll see her next." I keep my face neutral.

Go ahead, send me back, I dare you.

I give the door a satisfying slam as I leave. Dr. Ben would never believe I acted this way. It must be an effect from the wormhole radiation, or my exhausting day. Yeah, it's the latter, hopefully.

As I leave the human quarters, I think about what Aunt Katie said. I'll almost assuredly win a Nobel Prize, and probably before I'm thirty. I should probably be more accepting while I'm here. It wouldn't have gone so badly if Timberwolf wasn't there.

Oh. My. God. Could he become my uncle?

My head sinks and my whole body shakes. No, I have other problems to deal with, like if this future internationally renowned thought leader can remember how to get back to the others.

* * *

I hear the puppies barking up ahead. Once I catch up with Dingo, I breathe a sigh of relief. No one will find my decaying remains in some abandoned hallway. Not with all the noise these three are making.

Dingo is engrossed with the two dogs as they run circles around us. With a little time to think, my self-recriminations jump into high gear.

Did I just make enemies of the two most powerful people here?

According to my watch, I haven't even been here five hours yet and I'm mentally and physically exhausted. Tomorrow morning, after I get a good night's sleep, I'll try to see Aunt Katie and patch things up.

Nothing looks familiar to me, but then, every dimly lit hallway looks alike, so what do I know?

I open the door. "Lead the way," I say to the dogs, though they understand even less than Dingo.

The dogs go bursting through the doorway and don't stop until they turn the corner. The hackles raise on the two wiener dogs, and they let out a number of low growls, which I suppose are meant to be menacing rather than comical.

"Are these our dinner tonight?" Shadow asks as he turns the corner.

"No!" I say. "Let me explain."

I have no idea how to explain this.

Once inside, the dachshunds see a rolling Buddy and chase him around the room. Either everyone is amused, or else hungry. I'm *pretty* sure it's amusement, but why take chances?

"Everyone, these are my . . . good friend Dingo's pets." I nearly said mine, but Aunt Katie offered them to Dingo, not me.

"What are they called?" Shadow asks. Despite his overly masculine persona, he can't take his eyes off the puppies.

"They are dogs," I say. "We humans often keep them as pets."

"Play us no games,

What are their names?"

So Calliope is interested too.

"I defer to Dingo, since they are his."

Buddy has stopped rolling and walks up next to Dingo so we can understand each other. "They are enslaved to me?" Dingo asks, horrified.

"No, no, no," I say. "They are loving and playful creatures, but they are not capable of taking care of themselves here on the station. So you take care of their needs and they'll be happy to clown around like they are doing now. Everyone ends up happy."

"But I don't know any names," Dingo says. "You name them."

"Alright." I drop to my knees so I can pet the pooches. The short-haired one leans into me and gently licks the back of my hand. "Growing up, I had a friend who was really quiet and exceedingly kind. So I'll name this one Sebastian Carlisle." I scratch him above his tail.

The long-haired one sees me giving attention to someone other than him, and he is immediately aggrieved. He chases poor Sebastian away and jumps up, claws leading as he catches my thigh and rakes his claws down it.

I grab his front legs and drop them back to the floor.

"That one's called Barry–" I catch myself. I can't insult the dog by naming it after Dr. Barry Carter, even if it is wild-haired and obnoxiously loud. "His name is Dingle Barry." I can't help but smile. It's the perfect name for him.

Grendel lets out some subvocal grunts as she reaches for the dogs. Standing up, she has each dog sitting in one of her palms. Other than a tail wag, they are as docile as can be.

"Needed here," the Yeti says.

"Yes," Shadow says, "bring them tomorrow. They are of interest."

"They're Dingo's," I remind them. "Does that mean that Dingo should join us too?"

"Yesyesyes!" Buddy says.

I can't lie, I'm pretty pleased with myself. I've already started making bonds with the others. Now if I can only get along with the humans.

Dingo

Age:	< 1 year
Sex:	M
Species:	Napoleon/Bwetnib hybrid
Note:	Member of human contingent
Social Status / Rank:	Only known example
Height / Build:	2'8" (81.3 cm)
Weight:	65 lbs (29.5 kg)
Hair color:	Tan
Eyes color:	Black, four eyes
Marks/Tattoos:	None
Education / Training:	None
Skills/Talents:	None, grown in tank, get bio samples

Chapter Ten

After Duty Drinks

❖

Note to self, never ask Crighton, or any Napoleon, about creating forms, filling out forms or storing forms. My head feels like it's ready to explode, and honestly, I'd be okay with that. My eyes are blurry from all the digital signatures, thanks to the Dingo situation. I don't even want to think about getting Sebastian and Dingle Barry squared away on the station.

The U.S. military requires actual signatures, not digital ones. Aunt Katie saw to that. She gave each of the other species fountain pens when she first arrived, and now everyone must write out their names. Of course, they sign their names in their own scripts, so I don't see much use in it for the military. For me, it's another way to engage with them. Thank goodness for ridiculous bureaucracies, I guess.

Nothing Aunt Katie does surprises me anymore.

Dingo is leaning in next to me, trying to learn his new native language. He had Buddy stand between us, so we could communicate. I put a stop to that rancid breath assault by

150

calling out each letter, then pronouncing each word. Dingo is a quick study, and it's not long before he's announcing the letters as I write them. Still, it's tedious, time consuming, and he still has to consult Buddy every few of minutes. After one page, I have to stop, or else my brain will puree itself.

The others are entertaining the puppies. Shadow keeps flopping face down on the floor and making grunting noises while Buddy lets loose with high-pitched yips while he run-tumbles about the room. The dachshunds think it's great fun.

"Tim told us it is customary for humans to buy the first round after their initial shift is over," Shadow says while his butt is in the air and his head's resting on the floor.

"Hunger not at bay

Fasting for the day."

Just when I thought the day would end with only one interstellar incident.

"Guys, I just got off the spaceship minutes before this shift. All I have on me are United States of America dollars. I'm pretty sure they won't spend here."

"Showusan image!" Buddy says.

"I can do better than that." I pull out my wallet and take out the good ole American greenbacks. It's anachronistic, but I've always liked carrying cash.

"The men and women pictured here are all old leaders of my country." I fan the bills out and my colleagues grab for them at once.

A fifty drops to the ground and Dingle Barry snags it before I can. He runs off with it, only to have Sebastian catch him. The two play a disastrous game of tug of war. I try to grab hold of the bill but whiff as it's ripped in two. The puppies run to different corners and covetously eat their half of the bill. Clearly I'm the loser of this game.

Sixteen hundred dollars, gone in seconds, though it was going towards my rent, so . . ..

"This green bill,

Treasure I will."

"Wait, I just wanted to show you–"

"Ican'twait to show my parade mates! Iwillbe hero of my level."

"Green." Grendel says in her usual understated way.

"There is no policy that forbids currency in paper form. This will be brought up in the biweekly station free policy forum." Crighton's eyes twinkle. "Perhaps the drafting of another form will be needed."

"I need to get that back from y'all . . .." My words melt away.

"Gifts retaken

Giver forsaken."

"Yes, but . . .." I look around and realize I've lost already.

Grendel points up at the digital clock.

"The shift is over," Shadow says, "and Tim will be waiting for us."

Tim didn't mention that I'm buying drinks after the shift, or that the kleptos would take all my money. They better let me put the tab on credit.

* * *

The temporary human section is between the Yetis and the Erati sections. It was supposed to be a storage ring, but each spacefaring race has agreed to store some of the materials in their own areas. Because the ring was meant for storage, there are no windows on the human level and only half of the habitable areas have been fitted with human-appropriate lighting. I can already guess that my quarters won't be in one of the well-lit halls.

Matt, Trinity, and Hiram are at a standing table, so I lead my pack straight to them. Their looks of amazement are priceless. Trinity and Hiram try to flee, but Grendel tells them to stay. I'd like to see the person, of any species, that tells her no.

Shadow goes directly for Matt and they sniff each other, and I'm not being metaphorical. Buddy and Dingo, with the puppies in tow, head for Trinity. Hiram introduces himself to

153

Calliope, more out of desperation I think. Everyone's afraid of Grendel and no one wants to talk to Crighton, so they stand next to me, watching the greetings.

"Grendel, would you come with me?" I look up at her. "I'd like to ask those people if they'd let us have that larger table."

She smiles. An actual smile! Grendel, at least, likes me. An extra jolt of electricity flows through me. If I'm reading this right, which I am, I think . . . maybe.

The people melt away from the table before I can even ask. Grendel gives off a yodel, and the rest of the aliens and the humans, all of whom are my friends, join us.

Tim points at me from the bar and the whole group of humans laugh. Great, he's seducing my aunt and making me the butt of his jokes to people I haven't even met yet. Every superhero has their nemesis. All I need now are super powers.

Tim's holding a purple fizzy drink in a cocktail glass as he comes to greet us. It's been years since I've thrown a punch, but I'd love to knock that self-satisfied smirk off his face.

"I told you guys to take it easy on the newbie," he says as he and Shadow do some intricate handshake. Dingle Barry bites Tim's shoe, and he draws his foot back, as if to kick my dog.

Grendel kicks Buddy, and the Bwetnib takes out Tim's leg. Both he and his drink crash to the floor.

"Dingle Barry young," the Yeti says.

Tim dusts himself off, staring daggers at me—as if I had anything to do with it. Behind him, the crowd is laughing at him now.

Justice.

"Did you use your family connections to bring two dogs onto the station? Were you that desperate to have some friends here?" Tim asks, loud enough for everyone to hear.

"I don't know, *Timberwolf*," I reply just as loud. "Maybe you should ask the commandant during your pillow talk tonight."

Everyone freezes for an instant. Then Tim balls his fist. I block its trajectory with my face.

I feel my bottom lip and taste the warm blood. I look at him and smile. "I guess you wouldn't last long under interrogation."

Tim grabs my collar and lifts it into my neck. Before he can land a second punch, Grendel grabs his free arm. Tim turns away and sees the four women he was chatting with lean in to each other and whisper amongst themselves.

"If people haven't been impressed with your efforts lately," I say, "there's medication for that."

The tall blonde behind Tim spits out her drink. Belatedly, she tries to hide her laughter behind her hand. I wink at her.

Tim catches the exchange and clenches his teeth. With Grendel hovering, there's not much he can do. He juts his chin toward me and he stares me down for a long moment, then he returns to his spot at the bar.

Relieved, I touch my lip and draw away blood. Shadow is in my face and licking my bloody lip . . . and my teeth and my tongue. I pull away before he can reach my uvula. He grabs my hand as I try not to gag and licks the blood away from there, too.

I duck away from him and try to wipe his saliva off my lip and teeth, but it's already turned rubbery. I grab the plug of goo, but pulling on it will only tear my lip open. I cover my face with my hands to hide my sheer disgust.

Grendel emits a low rumble, which isn't translated, so I assume it's laughter. The Yeti pats me on my back, but softer this time. I'm in no danger of having a rib broken.

I stand up straight. "I'm okay now," I say to no one in particular.

I know I'll regret my action soon enough, but for now, I revel in the sweet taste of victory . . . and Umbran saliva.

"Um, Anthony," Matt says, "we're going to go."

I can't blame them. They don't need to be on Tim's enemy list.

"You really get around, don't you?" The brunette at the bar asks Tim. She and her friend—who has to be her twin—leave him. The blonde from earlier slides further away, not closer. His harem of four women is down to one.

Shadow's gloppy saliva has glued my lip to my bottom teeth, so my big, broad smile causes my cut lip to reopen.

"Big mistake, recruit," he says while wagging his finger at me. Back at the bar, he grabs the hand of the last remaining woman and drags her and her long black curls out of the bar.

Calliope saddles up to the bar.

"A meal for me

The first of three."

Grendel stands next to her and taps on the bar. Shadow picks Buddy up and sets him on a high seat. I reach for Crighton and he gives me a death glare. With his wee little arms and legs, the Napoleon scales the back of the chair and takes his place next to Buddy. I reach for Dingo instead.

"You paying for this?" The barkeep asks.

"Tim said to put it on his open tab," the blonde says.

I give her my best smile. This is the strangest of places, but that just means it will make an interesting home.

* * *

After Calliope puts away three meals, Grendel drinks two gallons of a two-tone neon green and orange drink and the rest snarf down food like they haven't eaten in two weeks. They finally take their leave. Dingo is napping on the floor and the two puppies are curled up against him. The bartender is busy polishing glasses with a dirty rag. I smile; can he be more of a *cliché?*

Most of the people have left for the evening, morning, whatever time it is. I'm only waiting on Wendy, the blonde that offered up Tim's tab, to return before I turn in. Here she comes now. I smile at her and she starts to return it, but then veers away from me.

What did I do?

My eyes follow her as she heads for the door, where Aunt Katie is standing. The colonel heads for me, so I down what's left of my drink as I wait. The green and orange concoction that Grendel loves so much is surprisingly good. The top layer is citrussy and sweet while the bottom is more herbal. I've never tasted either of these flavors, but the barkeep told me it's safe to drink.

"Alfred," Aunt Katie says. "You can close up for the night. I'll lock up."

"Yes ma'am," he says, dropping his rag in the bin.

At least I know it's nighttime.

Aunt Katie goes behind the bar and mixes up something for herself. She leans over the bar. "So last week you received your Ph.D. Do you have anything adventurous planned, now that you've earned your degree?"

My mouth drops open as I stare at this doppelgänger impersonating my 'by the book bitty' aunt, as Dad calls her.

She chuckles. "It's good to let your hair down every once in a while."

"Your hair is still up in a tight bun," is all I can say.

"We didn't do you any favors, the way we brought you here. And I have no doubt that General Poppycock did the absolute minimum to prepare you for the job at hand."

"You two don't get along?"

"Oh, we smile and nod and wish daggers into each other's hearts. It's the officer's way." She taps the bar a couple of times. "The truth be told, the service was getting ready to retire me. It's nothing less than a miracle that I was stationed at Groom Lake when Buddy arrived and invited us up here."

"You mean my Buddy, the one I work with?"

"The same. He showed up on the strip in Vegas. We mobilized immediately once we realized it was a first contact situation. He was more than happy to go back to our base. His complete lack of fear told us he's either a simpleton, or hopelessly advanced and not threatened by us," she says. "Perhaps a bit of both."

"How does the world not know about this if he landed in Vegas?" I ask.

"We told the media he was a costumed actor. He was approaching tourists instead of staying in his spot. That's a permit violation, so he was removed."

I shake my head. "Only in Vegas."

"Now, as for us, we've got off on the wrong foot."

"Yeah, I spoke without thinking."

"You've had quite the day, and I'm proud of you," Aunt Katie says. "You got more from our hosts in one shift than the rest of us were able to get in a month."

"Even a blind Napoleon will find the right form every now and then."

Aunt Katie just smiles and drinks her concoction. "When you go back to Earth, whenever that is, be leery of General Alexanders. She covets my job. Although she'll have to do better than trying to set off my allergies if she wants me to leave." She looks over at Dingo and the dogs, curled up under a table.

"I don't know that I'm cut out for the military life," I say.

"Let's get you and your *parade mates* to your quarters." With one final swig, she finishes her drink. "I don't know where you're going to take them to relieve themselves. It's not like we have a grassy field here."

"Aunt Katie, you're a genius. Tomorrow, I'm going to tell the guys about our sweeping meadows and mention that the grass will grow here with proper watering and lighting. If I tell Shadow we can play soccer on it, he'll be demanding we bring some grass seed up."

"I wasn't kidding when I said you'll win the Nobel Prize for this," she says in a low tone so Dingo and the puppies don't wake up. "Now get some sleep. You've got a busy day tomorrow.

I don't even want to know, though there's no chance it can be any more intense than today.

Thanks for reading my book!

Here are the five dogs I've had through the years
and the aliens inspired by them.

Please consider signing up for my newsletter or find out more about me and my works at: AuthorMikeMollman.Substack.com.

My friend and fellow author, Ro Bushey, and I have a YouTube channel: https://www.youtube.com/@Bald_and_Balding

For the rest of my social links, go to my linktree: https://linktr.ee/mikemollman

Finally, ratings and reviews are the social proof that we independent authors desperately need to stay relevant. Please consider leaving one for me or any other author you read.

ACKNOWLEDGEMENTS

The path to writing a book is a long and winding one. While much of the work is done alone, no one can finish a book worth reading without a lot of help.

My beta reader, Yar Gul, my editor, Rosaire Bushey, and my proofreader, Melissa Stone took my lump of a story and made it shine. I cannot recommend them highly enough. They can be found at:

https://www.fiverr.com/yargul?source=gig_page

https://www.rosairebushey.com/editing-services

https://www.fiverr.com/keverynn?source=order_page_summary_seller_link

Then there are those who provided services without payment.

There is only one person in this world that I could ask "Imagine you're the goddess of the pixies. How would you react if . . ." This person is Jeff Davidson, my agent of chaos. His imagination is unbounded.

My brother Danny had to listen to my trials and tribulations almost nightly, so I would be remiss not to mention him here.

He had an opinion for every question I'd put to him, and sometimes he was even helpful.

Dr. Wyatt Johnson, once asked me why we are friends. I told him it's because he makes poor decisions. This is the book he has been pushing me to publish for years now.

My nephew, Johnny Mollman M.D. was uncomfortable but very helpful in deciding exactly what wounds my characters could receive and still survive. Something about a hypocritical oath, or something.

OTHER BOOKS BY MIKE MOLLMAN

Proxima Station Saga

Book One: Proxima Station (2025)

*Book Two: Jungle Planet (2025, hopefully)

*Book Three: Area 51 Audit (tentative title, 2026)

*Book Four: TBD

*Book Five: TBD

*Book Six: TBD

The Martian Traders Saga

Book One: The Halley Traveler (2024)

*Book Two: Stranded And Alone (2025)

*Book Three: TBD

*Book Four: TBD

*Book Five   TBD

Protectors of Pretanni

Book One: Becoming A Druid (2021)

Book Two: Sins And Sorrows (2022)

Book Three: To Speak With Elders (2022)

Book Four: Desperate Dispatches (2024)

* Book Five: Becoming A King (2026)

* Book Six: Preparing For War

* Book Seven: The Return Of Loris

**Heirs to a Flawed Creation
E. L. Montague**

Purpose defines us. It will define the peoples we leave behind when we are gone. We are children playing with the powers of a god. Our creations will be as flawed as their creators. The gift of intellect comes with doubt.

In the none too distant future, tools will become beings in their own right. Factory floors will be the womb of an entire people. Androids will struggle to exist alongside the lesser gods who created them, even as they surpass us.

These stories explore that struggle.

The Sunset Sovereign
Laura Huie

For the past thousand years, the dragon Vakandi has watched the people of Vakfored grow from a wandering band of refugees to a glorious city of art and magic. Under his protection, the city has survived monsters, floods, and wars all without building an army, dam, or even a wall. But time changes everything and now the citizens of his beloved city want him dead.

Vakandi spends his last day telling his assassin why he loves them, and why it's his time to die.

Platinum Tinted Darkness

Timothy Wolff
The Kingdom of Boulom has been lost.

The realms have already seen what happens when the Gods and their Harbingers are left unchecked.
Destruction. Chaos. Death.

The Gods cannot be trusted. No one knows that better than David Williams, the leader of the Guardians tasked to protect the realm from the gods and their powerful Harbingers ever since the fall of Boulom.

Magic's Genesis: The Grey
Rosaire Bushey

When magic comes to Eigrae, an average woman becomes one of the most powerful people in the world, and a broken man becomes one of the most dangerous. For Lydria, learning to be a Wielder means trusting her friends, her own decisions, and accepting her role in a new world. For Wynter, the limits of magic are the limits of his own body. With direction from the voice of the woman he loved, the woman he killed, Wynter is pushed to rule without mercy, to bend Eigrae to his will, and remove those who defy him. In his quest to rule, he destroys what he must, and in the process creates a new species...dragons.

Shadow of Wolves
J. R. White

A tortured gunfighter. A Navajo outcast. – And the Creature whose claws would stain the stones of the Mojave red.

Flush with raw silver and ruled by a baron with an iron fist, the tiny mining outpost of Shank's Point is under siege by a sinister evil.

When the rising sun reveals the claw-torn bodies littered among the rocks, John Swift-Runner calls on his old friend, a vagabond gunfighter, to stand with him against the slaughter he knows will come.

But as their band of misfits hunts for the creature on the burning sands of the Mojave, they stumble into a generations old mystery that goes beyond shamanic curses and into the bloodstained pages of legend.

Can the killing be stopped?

Mike Mollman is a charming individual graced with good looks, undeniable charisma and humility. These descriptions come straight from his keyboard, so they must be treated as unimpeachable facts. Mike lives in the Richmond, Virginia area. When he's not self-aggrandizing, he likes to spend time with his two dogs and the many voices in his head.

www.ingramcontent.com/pod-product-compliance
Lightning Source LLC
Chambersburg PA
CBHW031751200726
48289CB00013B/789